LEO TOLSTOY

Stories and Legends

ILLUSTRATIONS BY ALEXANDER ALEXEIEFF

TRANSLATION BY LOUISE AND AYLMER MAUDE

INTRODUCTION BY DOROTHY CANFIELD FISHER

PANTHEON BOOKS INC. NEW YORK

Manufactured in the U. S. A. by H. Wolff, New York, for
PANTHEON BOOKS INC.
41 Washington Square, New York, N. Y.

CONTENTS

INTRODUCTION

BY DOROTHY CANFIELD FISHER

WHY should a publisher present the reading public with yet another collection of stories selected from the folktales of Tolstoy? Why should an American author of the twentieth-century accept as an honor the chance to write something about such a volume? There are plenty of other editions where Tolstoy's fables can be found. For more than sixty years, the printing presses of the world have issued and re-issued them in many languages. There is no need to "introduce" them. People of many races, with hair now quite white, looking back towards their 'teens, recall the very look of the chairs and tables and windows and walls of the room in which they read, for the never-to-be-forgotten first time, this one or that of these stories, and looking up from the book, found themselves out of childhood, deep in the timeless realm of the spirit. Nor is there any need to rescue them from oblivion. They have been our intimates for a long, long time, but never gone from the memory of mankind. The "terrible gift of familiarity" has never hidden their beauty, so full of strong and tender meaning, from our fickle human eyes.

Why then—? The answer to that "why" is with another "why"? Why does a good mother set bread upon the table

7

for her family today? They had bread yesterday, the week before, the year before. Yes, but they need it, day by day. The younger ones must have it as food for their growth. Those in the prime of their years must have it as basis for the strength to carry the burden of responsibility and authority which is the lot of the mature. The old—who have in their long lives already eaten so much bread—still need it, as a protection from too-rapid failing of the physical powers—threat to that ripening of the spiritual understanding which is the reward of age, recompense for its bodily ills. Well, Tolstoy's folk-tales and fables are bread of the spirit. They are not just anecdotes to be read once—or at most, twice—and then no more, because now the reader knows what happened in that story. Everyone sees more in them as his heart and mind expand to take in more of truth illimitable. The reader of forty, with two decades of grown-up life back of him sees something more imperiously true in the mighty tale called "God sees the truth but waits," than that which at sixteen so powerfully, perhaps painfully, moved his rebellious boy heart. The old woman of seventy reading again "Where Love is, God is" finds on its margins written in the invisible ink of memory, passages from her own life confirming its wisdom.

And like bread, they must constantly be kept upon the table of mankind, now in this form, now in that, ready to the seeking hand of youth, of maturity, of age. What this new volume does is to present a new selection, carefully chosen to blend with each other in one whole, to make one harmonizing impression on the twentieth-century reader—young or older.

Was there ever a period of human history when the children of man more needed the spiritual food spread before them in these true stories? (Yes, true, even when a winged angel is part of one, actually far truer than anything photographically

8

literal.) For these are stories of love and its sunny, boundless power; and we are living in the reek of hate. What is always reflected from the dark mirror of hate—resentment, rage, and retaliation, fill our hearts with poison.

These narratives of what love can do for human beings are so permeated with the spirit of love that even now in the hour of our deadly peril we do not react to them with a protest as we do to so many exhortations to peaceful ways. There is in their clarity no trace—not even a subconscious tinge—of that blame for those who know not love, which so strangely marks with self-righteousness (so at least many of us feel) the exhortations to peace and love of some modern moralists. They are timeless, fruit ripened to full maturity on the tree of the spirit. They present no raw, easily refuted, specific recipe for freeing ourselves from the blind labyrinth of murder in which we rush to and fro, vainly seeking escape. At no point do they give us reason for the frantic self-defensive outcry of "How can we do anything else but fight—*now?*" with which we repel other suggestions, which seem to us absurdly and tragically impractical, to leave off hating and learn to love. Tolstoy reminds us peaceably—not belligerently—of peace. He does not say "Do this one thing, or that other thing as I tell you to, and then you could stop fighting and hating." We know very well that we cannot escape from the hideous abyss into which we, with all our human brothers, have fallen, where we struggle and suffer, by "doing" any one thing. We need no sermonizing to inform us that what we are all doing is wrong. Since most of us honestly do not see how—now, as things are—we can stop doing a present wrong without risking the whole future of what we think is right, we bitterly resent what seems to us empty words. To tell us that our intolerable misery is self-inflicted is to mock us; as if a passer-by stopping by a man with

9

a broken leg, should tell him, severely, "if you had not lost your way in the fog and fallen from that rock, you would still be whole and sound, and able to go forward on your way."

Tolstoy's spirit of love is the sunshine which rolls the fog up like a curtain, and shows us the human landscape, green and gold and fertile and rewarding. In its light we see for ourselves where we left the path, where catastrophe followed on our misstep. We see that there is a right path, we follow with our eyes where it winds off through fields of grain, shaded woodlands, and orchards of fruit, to tranquil homes where our children could live safely. He does not tell us in complacent detail how to better our present plight. Indeed he does not so much as mention it. But as we read him, we are moved to lift our eyes and see that, for all our wretchedness, what we are now living through is only a part of an infinitely greater whole. Tolstoy's portrayal of the joy of men when they love and serve each other gives us a thousand times more reason to live on, to recover our health, to help our children learn, better than we ever did, how to walk in the calm creative ways of peace.

But—it comes to us with a start of surprise,—we realize that all of this is in innumerable sermons. How does it happen that Tolstoy and not the preachers can reach our hearts with this reminder that peace and love are beautiful beyond words, and that we can have peace and love if we will deserve those blessings? The answer is simple:—Tolstoy was a great artist.

When Tolstoy began writing his folk-stories he was at his prime both in experience of human life and in the practice of his art. He had lived through most of what life can bring to man—with the exception of poverty and crime—and those shadows he had known with his seer's divination. He had been an army officer in active warfare. He had seen at first hand the wild, free life of nomad tribes. He was an accepted familiar

10

in the most formally aristocratic society. He had for years lived close to the soil, as a farmer. He had known love, marriage, fatherhood, joy, racking sorrow—five of his children had died in their early youth under his roof, in his arms. As an author he had achieved as great a distinction, as wide a fame as any author of his century. From the profusion of these riches, he distilled a clear essential simplicity and poured it into his tales for the young and for the pure of heart.

His great novels had made him famous for many extraordinary literary skills, but pre-eminently for one,—that his characters live. The reader does not think of them as inventions of an author. They are his brother-men. This miracle Tolstoy accomplished partly by his divination of the hidden inner life in each human being, and partly by a magical power of evocation in the use of detail. You know and share to your very heart what a man or woman in one of his books is secretly feeling and you also see him, as in the very flesh,—see the special way he takes hold of a chair to move it, see the personal mannerisms of movement of a woman putting the hairpins into her hair, see the specific, individual curve of her hand as she leans towards a table to pick up a book, see the idiosyncrasy of gesture, not like that of other men, in which a man lights a cigar, coughs, turns his head, drops his eyes. Having seen him in the flesh, over and over, knowing far more than those about him ever know of what he really hopes, fears, longs for, sorrows over, he is a living person to you. What happens to him, really happens. You cannot but believe that it happens.

This magician's skill Tolstoy fully possessed when, in his fifties he turned from his great, complex symphonic compositions, to writing fables. He held his tools as the master workman does, with light easy certainty. The phase of intoxicated delight in his disciplined genius was behind him. He used his great powers sparingly, a touch here, a touch there, enough

11

to bring out the design, never enough to hide the true nature of the material he was shaping.

Because there is no rich-blooming exuberance of description as in the novels, because for the most part you see the plain, grave, simplicity of human life in its essence, the reader's attention is free to enjoy with a sort of ecstasy the exact rightness of the relatively few details Tolstoy selects. Examples could be taken from any page of any one of the tales. To choose one at random,—no, not at random, one of the most difficult ones for a modern reader to feel at home with—some details may be cited in the strange story of the archangel Michael, entitled "What Men Live By." The plot of the story is known to everyone who has ever in his childhood had a pious elderly relative read aloud to him from a collection of "Lives of the Saints." He yawned and wriggled and looked yearningly at the clock, bored with the silly fairy-tale of an archangel who, for disobeying one of God's commands, was punished by being made to live as a human being for a while. When, at the end, after many queer actions, the angel sprouted wings and flew back to heaven, the young listener slid from his chair and rushed back to play, Gabriel or Michael ranking in his mind far below Jack the Giant-killer.

In the Tolstoy story, the use of detail, sober and sure, laid on with an inspired choice, takes you out of the life you know, and as if in literal fact, into the low-ceilinged hut of the shoemaker: "Michael gathered up the remnants of the leather; rolled them up, took the soft slippers he had made, slapped them together, wiped them down with his apron, and handed them and the roll of leather to the servant, who took them and said: 'Good-bye, masters, and good day to you!' " Were you not there? Did you not see Michael, the good workman, hand over the slippers he had made to the wealthy man's servant? Did you not hear the slap with which he freed them from dust;

12

smell the rich odor from the fine leather such as the poor cobbler rarely handled?

Sometimes the detail is so slight as to be noticeable only in the most microscopic observation, yet magically evocative. In the same story the children inside the shoemaker's house are playing noisily together, the mother is rattling iron pots, the workman so strangely oblivious to all about him is hammering nails into a shoe heel. Suddenly he stops short, and for the first time since he had worked for Simon, threw down his work to stare intently out of the window. Amazed, they all looked, too, and see a well-dressed woman with two little girls coming to the hut. Can it be a customer coming to give a much hoped-for order? Why should Michael stop his work to stare at her? Tolstoy does not need to write a clever description of the suspense felt by the family inside the room; he does not need to say in so many literal words that their noise and clatter is struck into motionless silence by their wonder. He writes, in the simplest words, "The woman stepped into the porch outside and entered the passage. *Feeling about for the entrance, she found the latch, which she lifted and opened the door.* She let the two little girls go first and followed them into the hut. 'Good day, good folk' she said."

You, the reader, do not need to have the author remind you that they could have heard the light brushing of her fingers as she fumbled for the latch only if they had all—so active and noisily bustling the moment before—held their breath in listening silence. No, as you hear the faint sound of those groping fingers you are in the hushed room yourself, holding your own breath in suspense. By the skillful, delicately discreet but inspired choice of such details, the reader lives in the house with Michael, seeing, handling, tasting, smelling, hearing, feeling what goes on around him. He cannot but believe that it is all happening, there before his eyes, just as Tolstoy sets it down.

13

So that at the last, when the angel is clothed in light so that the eye cannot look on him, when wings appear on his shoulders, when he rises into the skies, you too, the reader, as well as the shoemaker and his family, bow in reverence.

Sometimes the detail is not minute and perfect, as in the instance of the hand fumbling for the latch, but momentous and perfect—though always of a folk-simplicity—sweeping you, like a change of key in a musical composition, from one plane of feeling to another. This happens in "Two Old Men." The rich man returning from his pilgrimage to Jerusalem goes into the hut where his poorer comrade, stopping for a drink of water, stayed to spend himself in saving a family's life. Till then the story has been the plainest, most matter-of-fact narrative. You see it all as what happened to one individual man, to one identifiable family. But as the old grandmother tells the tale to the new-comer: 'And just think what he did! As soon as he saw us, he let down his bag, on this very spot, and untied it.'

"Here the little girl joined in. 'No, Granny,' said she, 'first he put it down here in the middle of the hut, and then he lifted it on to the bench.' And they began discussing and recalling all he had said and done, where he sat and slept, and what he had said to each of them."

There, before your eyes you see a fact grow and flower into a folk-legend, because the fact has universal significance. It is breath-taking.

In none of these stories does Tolstoy's amazing command of factual detail play a greater part than in the masterpiece called "Master and Man." The sublimity of the master's ecstasy as he dies, is upheld by the massive density of his naturalistic materialism until then. Just so the soaring ecstasy of interlacing curves in the lofty Gothic arches of a great cathedral are upheld by the solid, straight-standing density of the pillars,

14

one stone piled squarely on top of the one below it, in the oldest and simplest of man's devices for supporting roofs.

There are even "timely" considerations, connected factually with the news of the day, which make it well to call to the attention of American readers a new collection of Tolstoy's stories of loving-kindness. One of these is the veneration shown for him by modern Russians, as they prove by making a museum-shrine out of his house. We do not think of Soviet Russia as a religious-minded country,—quite the contrary. Yet Tolstoy's old house was kept by official government decree exactly as it was when he lived there, the very furniture—so far as possible —in the places where it stood when that mighty pen was held in the old master's hand, the rickety table still standing where his devoted wife toiled at copying the books, the spirit of which she so little understood.

We Americans had, most of us, taken this official recognition for granted. What else save affection could any people, able to read and write, feel for Tolstoy? The greatness of his soul, the magnificent achievements of his literary genius far transcended, we thought, any differing political economic theories. It did not occur to us—most of us—that the quality of a nation's character is wordlessly depicted in the heroes it chooses to admire. In our interpretation of the character of Soviet Russia, we quite forgot to include the fact that it made a place of pilgrimage out of the scene where Tolstoy had suffered as he fought with himself to turn away from materialism—pleasant, kind, and unoffending though his was—and to seek out loving-kindness.

To do homage to greatness of heart is possible only to the great-hearted. Goodness cannot be loved by those who do evil wilfully. From the spirit of love, as from Tolstoy's angel, ever shines a brightness as from summer lightning upon all those who reverence it.

15

What Men Live By

"*We know that we have passed out of death unto life, because we love the brethren. He that loveth not abideth in death.*"—1 Epistle St. John iii. 14.

"*Whoso hath the world's goods, and beholdeth his brother in need, and shutteth up his compassion from him, how doth the love of God abide in him? My little children, let us not love in word, neither with the tongue; but in deed and truth.*"—iii. 17-18.

"*Love is of God; and every one that loveth is begotten of God, and knoweth God. He that loveth not knoweth not God; for God is love.*" —iv. 7-8.

"*No man hath beheld God at any time; if we love one another, God abideth in us.*"— iv. 12.

"*God is love; and he that abideth in love abideth in God, and God abideth in him.*"— iv. 16.

"*If a man say, I love God, and hateth his brother, he is a liar; for he that loveth not his brother whom he hath seen, how can he love God whom he hath not seen?*"—iv. 20.

A SHOEMAKER named Simon, who had neither house
nor land of his own, lived with his wife and children in
a peasant's hut and earned his living by his work. Work was
cheap but bread was dear, and what he earned he spent for

food. The man and his wife had but one sheep-skin coat between them for winter wear, and even that was worn to tatters, and this was the second year he had been wanting to buy sheep-skins for a new coat. Before winter Simon saved up a little money: a three-rúble note lay hidden in his wife's box, and five rúbles and twenty kopéks [1] were owed him by customers in the village.

So one morning he prepared to go to the village to buy the sheep-skins. He put on over his shirt his wife's wadded nankeen jacket, and over that he put his own cloth coat. He took the three-rúble note in his pocket, cut himself a stick to serve as a staff, and started off after breakfast. "I'll collect the five rúbles that are due to me," thought he, "add the three I have got, and that will be enough to buy sheep-skins for the winter coat."

He came to the village and called at a peasant's hut, but the man was not at home. The peasant's wife promised that the money should be paid next week, but she would not pay it herself. Then Simon called on another peasant, but this one swore he had no money, and would only pay twenty kopéks which he owed for a pair of boots Simon had mended. Simon then tried to buy the sheep-skins on credit, but the dealer would not trust him.

"Bring your money," said he, "then you may have your pick of the skins. We know what debt-collecting is like."

So all the business the shoemaker did was to get the twenty kopéks for boots he had mended, and to take a pair of felt boots a peasant gave him to sole with leather.

Simon felt downhearted. He spent the twenty kopéks on vódka, and started homewards without having bought any skins. In the morning he had felt the frost; but now, after drinking the vódka, he felt warm even without a sheep-skin coat.

[1] One hundred kopéks make a rúble. The rúble is worth about fifty cents; the kopék about half a cent.

20

He trudged along, striking his stick on the frozen earth with one hand, swinging the felt boots with the other, and talking to himself.

"I'm quite warm," said he, "though I have no sheep-skin coat. I've had a drop and it runs through all my veins. I need no sheep-skins. I go along and don't worry about anything. That's the sort of man I am! What do I care? I can live without sheep-skins. I don't need them. My wife will fret, to be sure. And, true enough, it *is* a shame; one works all day long and then does not get paid. Stop a bit! If you don't bring that money along, sure enough I'll skin you, blessed if I don't. How's that? He pays twenty kopéks at a time! What can I do with twenty kopéks? Drink it—that's all one can do! Hard up, he says he is! So he may be—but what about me? You have house, and cattle, and everything; I've only what I stand up in! You have corn of your own growing, I have to buy every grain. Do what I will, I must spend three rúbles every week for bread alone. I come home and find the bread all used up and I have to fork out another rúble and a half. So just you pay up what you owe, and no nonsense about it!"

By this time he had nearly reached the shrine at the bend of the road. Looking up, he saw something whitish behind the shrine. The daylight was fading, and the shoemaker peered at the thing without being able to make out what it was. "There was no white stone here before. Can it be an ox? It's not like an ox. It has a head like a man, but it's too white; and what could a man be doing there?"

He came closer, so that it was clearly visible. To his surprise it really was a man, alive or dead, sitting naked, leaning motionless against the shrine. Terror seized the shoemaker, and he thought, "Some one has killed him, stripped him, and left him here. If I meddle I shall surely get into trouble."

So the shoemaker went on. He passed in front of the shrine

21

so that he could not see the man. When he had gone some way he looked back, and saw that the man was no longer leaning against the shrine, but was moving as if looking towards him. The shoemaker felt more frightened than before, and thought, "Shall I go back to him or shall I go on? If I go near him something dreadful may happen. Who knows who the fellow is? He has not come here for any good. If I go near him he may jump up and throttle me, and there will be no getting away. Or if not, he'd still be a burden on one's hands. What could I do with a naked man? I couldn't give him my last clothes. Heaven only help me to get away!"

So the shoemaker hurried on, leaving the shrine behind him —when suddenly his conscience smote him and he stopped in the road.

"What are you doing, Simon?" said he to himself. "The man may be dying of want, and you slip past afraid. Have you grown so rich as to be afraid of robbers? Ah, Simon, shame on you!"

So he turned back and went up to the man.

II

Simon approached the stranger, looked at him, and saw that he was a young man, fit, with no bruises on his body, but evidently freezing and frightened, and he sat there leaning back without looking up at Simon, as if too faint to lift his eyes. Simon went close to him and then the man seemed to wake up. Turning his head, he opened his eyes and looked into Simon's face. That one look was enough to make Simon fond of the man. He threw the felt boots on the ground, undid his sash, laid it on the boots, and took off his cloth coat.

"It's not a time for talking," said he. "Come, put this coat on at once!" And Simon took the man by the elbows and helped him to rise. As he stood there, Simon saw that his body was

22

clean and in good condition, his hands and feet shapely, and his face good and kind. He threw his coat over the man's shoulders, but the latter could not find the sleeves. Simon guided his arms into them, and drawing the coat well on, wrapped it closely about him, tying the sash round the man's waist.

Simon even took off his torn cap to put it on the man's head, but then his own head felt cold and he thought: "I'm quite bald, while he has long curly hair." So he put his cap on his own head again. "It will be better to give him something for his feet," thought he; and he made the man sit down and helped him to put on the felt boots, saying, "There, friend, now move about and warm yourself. Other matters can be settled later on. Can you walk?"

The man stood up and looked kindly at Simon, but could not say a word.

"Why don't you speak?" said Simon. "It's too cold to stay here, we must be getting home. There now, take my stick, and if you're feeling weak lean on that. Now step out!"

The man started walking and moved easily, not lagging behind.

As they went along, Simon asked him, "And where do you belong to?"

"I'm not from these parts."

"I thought as much. I know the folks hereabouts. But how did you come to be there by the shrine?"

"I cannot tell."

"Has some one been ill-treating you?"

"No one has ill-treated me. God has punished me."

"Of course God rules all. Still, you'll have to find food and shelter somewhere. Where do you want to go to?"

"It is all the same to me."

Simon was amazed. The man did not look like a rogue, and he spoke gently, but yet he gave no account of himself. Still

23

Simon thought, "Who knows what may have happened?" And he said to the stranger: "Well then, come home with me and at least warm yourself awhile."

So Simon walked towards his home, and the stranger kept up with him, walking at his side. The wind had risen and Simon felt it cold under his shirt. He was getting over his tipsiness by now and began to feel the frost. He went along sniffling and wrapping his wife's jacket round him, and he thought to himself: "There now—talk about sheep-skins! I went out for sheep-skins and come home without even a coat to my back, and what is more, I'm bringing a naked man along with me. Matrëna won't be pleased!" And when he thought of his wife he felt sad; but when he looked at the stranger and remembered how he had looked up at him at the shrine, his heart was glad.

III

Simon's wife had everything ready early that day. She had cut wood, brought water, fed the children, eaten her own meal, and now she sat thinking. She wondered when she ought to make bread: now or to-morrow? There was still a large piece left.

"If Simon has had some dinner in town," thought she, "and does not eat much for supper, the bread will last out another day."

She weighed the piece of bread in her hand again and again, and thought: "I won't make any more to-day. We have only enough flour left to bake one batch. We can manage to make this last out till Friday."

So Matrëna put away the bread, and sat down at the table to patch her husband's shirt. While she worked she thought how her husband was buying skins for a winter coat.

"If only the dealer does not cheat him. My good man is

much too simple; he cheats nobody, but any child can take him in. Eight rúbles is a lot of money—he should get a good coat at that price. Not tanned skins, but still a proper winter coat. How difficult it was last winter to get on without a warm coat. I could neither get down to the river nor go out anywhere. When he went out he put on all we had, and there was nothing left for me. He did not start very early to-day, but still it's time he was back. I only hope he has not gone on the spree!"

Hardly had Matrëna thought this than steps were heard on the threshold and some one entered. Matrëna stuck her needle into her work and went out into the passage. There she saw two men: Simon, and with him a man without a hat and wearing felt boots.

Matrëna noticed at once that her husband smelt of spirits. "There now, he has been drinking," thought she. And when she saw that he was coatless, had only her jacket on, brought no parcel, stood there silent, and seemed ashamed, her heart was ready to break with disappointment. "He has drunk the money," thought she, "and has been on the spree with some good-for-nothing fellow whom he has brought home with him."

Matrëna let them pass into the hut, followed them in, and saw that the stranger was a young, slight man, wearing her husband's coat. There was no shirt to be seen under it, and he had no hat. Having entered, he stood neither moving nor rais- ing his eyes, and Matrëna thought: "He must be a bad man— he's afraid."

Matrëna frowned, and stood beside the stove looking to see what they would do.

Simon took off his cap and sat down on the bench as if things were all right.

"Come, Matrëna; if supper is ready, let us have some."

Matrëna muttered something to herself and did not move, but stayed where she was, by the stove. She looked first at the

25

one and then at the other of them and only shook her head. Simon saw that his wife was annoyed, but tried to pass it off. Pretending not to notice anything, he took the stranger by the arm.

"Sit down, friend," said he, "and let us have some supper."

The stranger sat down on the bench.

"Haven't you cooked anything for us?" said Simon.

Matrëna's anger boiled over. "I've cooked, but not for you. It seems to me you have drunk your wits away. You went to buy a sheep-skin coat, but come home without so much as the coat you had on, and bring a naked vagabond home with you. I have no supper for drunkards like you."

"That's enough, Matrëna. Don't wag your tongue without reason! You had better ask what sort of man——"

"And you tell me what you've done with the money?"

Simon found the pocket of the jacket, drew out the three-rúble note, and unfolded it.

"Here is the money. Trífonov did not pay, but promises to pay soon."

Matrëna got still more angry; he had bought no sheep-skins, but had put his only coat on some naked fellow and had even brought him to their house.

She snatched up the note from the table, took it to put away in safety, and said: "I have no supper for you. We can't feed all the naked drunkards in the world."

"There now, Matrëna, hold your tongue a bit. First hear what a man has to say——!"

"Much wisdom I shall hear from a drunken fool. I was right in not wanting to marry you—a drunkard. The linen my mother gave me you drank; and now you've been to buy a coat—and have drunk it too!"

Simon tried to explain to his wife that he had only spent twenty kopéks; tried to tell how he had found the man—but

26

Matrëna would not let him get a word in. She talked nineteen to the dozen, and dragged in things that had happened ten years before.

Matrëna talked and talked, and at last she flew at Simon and seized him by the sleeve.

"Give me my jacket. It is the only one I have, and you must needs take it from me and wear it yourself. Give it here, you mangy dog, and may the devil take you."

Simon began to pull off the jacket, and turned a sleeve of it inside out; Matrëna seized the jacket and it burst its seams. She snatched it up, threw it over her head and went to the door. She meant to go out, but stopped undecided—she wanted to work off her anger, but she also wanted to learn what sort of a man the stranger was.

I V

Matrëna stopped and said: "If he were a good man he would not be naked. Why, he hasn't even a shirt on him. If he were all right, you would say where you came across the fellow."

"That's just what I am trying to tell you," said Simon. "As I came to the shrine I saw him sitting all naked and frozen. It isn't quite the weather to sit about naked! God sent me to him or he would have perished. What was I to do? How do we know what may have happened to him? So I took him, clothed him, and brought him along. Don't be so angry, Matrëna. It is a sin. Remember, we must all die one day."

Angry words rose to Matrëna's lips, but she looked at the stranger and was silent. He sat on the edge of the bench, motionless, his hands folded on his knees, his head drooping on his breast, his eyes closed, and his brows knit as if in pain. Matrëna was silent, and Simon said: "Matrëna, have you no love of God?"

27

Matrëna heard these words, and as she looked at the stranger, suddenly her heart softened towards him. She came back from the door, and going to the stove she got out the supper. Setting a cup on the table, she poured out some *kvas*.[1] Then she brought out the last piece of bread and set out a knife and spoons.

"Eat, if you want to," said she.

Simon drew the stranger to the table.

"Take your place, young man," said he.

Simon cut the bread, crumbled it into the broth, and they began to eat. Matrëna sat at the corner of the table, resting her head on her hand and looking at the stranger.

And Matrëna was touched with pity for the stranger and began to feel fond of him. And at once the stranger's face lit up; his brows were no longer bent, he raised his eyes and smiled at Matrëna.

When they had finished supper, the woman cleared away the things and began questioning the stranger. "Where are you from?" said she.

"I am not from these parts."

"But how did you come to be on the road?"

"I may not tell."

"Did some one rob you?"

"God punished me."

"And you were lying there naked?"

"Yes, naked and freezing. Simon saw me and had pity on me. He took off his coat, put it on me, and brought me here. And you have fed me, given me drink, and shown pity on me. God will reward you!"

Matrëna rose, took from the window Simon's old shirt she had been patching, and gave it to the stranger. She also brought out a pair of trousers for him.

[1] A non-intoxicating drink usually made from rye-malt and rye-flour.

28

"There," said she, "I see you have no shirt. Put this on, and lie down where you please, in the loft or on the stove." [1]

The stranger took off the coat, put on the shirt, and lay down in the loft. Matrëna put out the candle, took the coat, and climbed to where her husband lay on the stove.

Matrëna drew the skirts of the coat over her and lay down but could not sleep; she could not get the stranger out of her mind.

When she remembered that he had eaten their last piece of bread and that there was none for to-morrow, and thought of the shirt and trousers she had given away, she felt grieved; but when she remembered how he had smiled, her heart was glad.

Long did Matrëna lie awake, and she noticed that Simon also was awake—he drew the coat towards him.

"Simon!"

"Well?"

"You have had the last of the bread and I have not put any to rise. I don't know what we shall do to-morrow. Perhaps I can borrow some of neighbor Martha."

"If we're alive we shall find something to eat."

The woman lay still awhile, and then said, "He seems a good man, but why does he not tell us who he is?"

"I suppose he has his reasons."

"Simon!"

"Well?"

"We give; but why does nobody give us anything?"

Simon did not know what to say; so he only said, "Let us stop talking," and turned over and went to sleep.

---

[1] The brick stove, including the oven, in a Russian peasant's hut is usually built so as to leave a flat top, large enough to lie on, for those who want to sleep in a warm place.

V

In the morning Simon awoke. The children were still asleep; his wife had gone to the neighbor's to borrow some bread. The stranger alone was sitting on the bench, dressed in the old shirt and trousers, and looking upwards. His face was brighter than it had been the day before.

Simon said to him, "Well, friend; the belly wants bread and the naked body clothes. One has to work for a living. What work do you know?"

"I do not know any."

This surprised Simon, but he said, "Men who want to learn can learn anything."

"Men work and I will work also."

"What is your name?"

"Michael."

"Well, Michael, if you don't wish to talk about yourself, that is your own affair; but you'll have to earn a living for yourself. If you will work as I tell you, I will give you food and shelter."

"May God reward you! I will learn. Show me what to do."

Simon took yarn, put it round his thumb and began to twist it.

"It is easy enough—see!"

Michael watched him, put some yarn round his own thumb in the same way, caught the knack, and twisted the yarn also.

Then Simon showed him how to wax the thread. This also Michael mastered. Next Simon showed him how to twist the bristle in, and how to sew, and this, too, Michael learned at once.

Whatever Simon showed him he understood at once, and after three days he worked as if he had sewn boots all his life. He worked without stopping and ate little. When work was over he sat silently, looking upwards. He hardly went into the

30

street, spoke only when necessary, and neither joked nor laughed. They never saw him smile, except that first evening when Matrëna gave them supper.

VI

Day by day and week by week the year went round. Michael lived and worked with Simon. His fame spread till people said that no one sewed boots so neatly and strongly as Simon's workman, Michael; from all the district round people came to Simon for their boots, and he began to be well off.

One winter day, as Simon and Michael sat working, a carriage on sledge-runners, with three horses and with bells, drove up to the hut. They looked out of the window; the carriage stopped at their door, a fine servant jumped down from the box and opened the door. A gentleman in a fur coat got out and walked up to Simon's hut. Up jumped Matrëna and opened the door wide. The gentleman stooped to enter the hut, and when he drew himself up again his head nearly reached the ceiling and he seemed quite to fill his end of the room.

Simon rose, bowed, and looked at the gentleman with astonishment. He had never seen any one like him. Simon himself was lean, Michael was thin, and Matrëna was dry as a bone, but this man was like some one from another world: red-faced, burly, with a neck like a bull's, and looking altogether as if he were cast in iron.

The gentleman puffed, threw off his fur coat, sat down on the bench, and said, "Which of you is the master bootmaker?"

"I am, your Excellency," said Simon, coming forward.

Then the gentleman shouted to his lad, "Hey, Fédka, bring the leather!"

The servant ran in, bringing a parcel. The gentleman took the parcel and put it on the table.

31

"Untie it," said he. The lad untied it.

The gentleman pointed to the leather.

"Look here, shoemaker," said he, "do you see this leather?"

"Yes, your Honor."

"But do you know what sort of leather it is?"

Simon felt the leather and said, "It is good leather."

"Good, indeed! Why, you fool, you never saw such leather before in your life. It's German, and cost twenty rúbles."

Simon was frightened, and said, "Where should I ever see leather like that?"

"Just so! Now, can you make it into boots for me?"

"Yes, your Excellency, I can."

Then the gentleman shouted at him: "You *can*, can you? Well, remember whom you are to make them for, and what the leather is. You must make me boots that will wear for a year, neither losing shape nor coming unsewn. If you can do it, take the leather and cut it up; but if you can't, say so. I warn you now, if your boots come unsewn or lose shape within a year I will have you put in prison. If they don't burst or lose shape for a year, I will pay you ten rúbles for your work."

Simon was frightened and did not know what to say. He glanced at Michael and, nudging him with his elbow, whispered: "Shall I take the work?"

Michael nodded his head as if to say, "Yes, take it."

Simon did as Michael advised and undertook to make boots that would not lose shape or split for a whole year.

Calling his servant, the gentleman told him to pull the boot off his left leg, which he stretched out.

"Take my measure!" said he.

Simon stitched a paper measure seventeen inches long, smoothed it out, knelt down, wiped his hands well on his apron so as not to soil the gentleman's sock, and began to measure. He measured the sole, and round the instep, and began to

32

measure the calf of the leg, but the paper was too short. The calf of the leg was as thick as a beam.

"Mind you don't make it too tight in the leg."

Simon stitched on another strip of paper. The gentleman twitched his toes about in his sock looking round at those in the hut, and as he did so he noticed Michael.

"Whom have you there?" asked he.

"That is my workman. He will sew the boots."

"Mind," said the gentleman to Michael, "remember to make them so that they will last me a year."

Simon also looked at Michael, and saw that Michael was not looking at the gentleman, but was gazing into the corner behind the gentleman, as if he saw some one there. Michael looked and looked, and suddenly he smiled, and his face became brighter.

"What are you grinning at, you fool?" thundered the gentleman. "You had better look to it that the boots are ready in time."

"They shall be ready in good time," said Michael.

"Mind it is so," said the gentleman, and he put on his boots and his fur coat, wrapped the latter round him, and went to the door. But he forgot to stoop, and struck his head against the lintel.

He swore and rubbed his head. Then he took his seat in the carriage and drove away.

When he had gone, Simon said: "There's a figure of a man for you! You could not kill him with a mallet. He almost knocked out the lintel, but little harm it did him."

And Matrëna said: "Living as he does, how should he not grow strong? Death itself can't touch such a rock as that."

VII

Then Simon said to Michael: "Well, we have taken the work, but we must see we don't get into trouble over it. The leather

33

is dear, and the gentleman hot-tempered. We must make no mistakes. Come, your eye is truer and your hands have become nimbler than mine, so you take this measure and cut out the boots. I will finish off the sewing of the vamps."

Michael did as he was told. He took the leather, spread it out on the table, folded it in two, took a knife and began to cut out.

Matrëna came and watched him cutting, and was surprised to see how he was doing it. Matrëna was accustomed to seeing boots made, and she looked and saw that Michael was not cutting the leather for boots, but was cutting it round.

She wished to say something, but she thought to herself: "Perhaps I do not understand how gentlemen's boots should be made. I suppose Michael knows more about it—and I won't interfere."

When Michael had cut up the leather he took a thread and began to sew not with two ends, as boots are sewn, but with a single end, as for soft slippers.

Again Matrëna wondered, but again she did not interfere. Michael sewed on steadily till noon. Then Simon rose for dinner, looked around, and saw that Michael had made slippers out of the gentleman's leather.

"Ah!" groaned Simon, and he thought, "How is it that Michael, who has been with me a whole year and never made a mistake before, should do such a dreadful thing? The gentleman ordered high boots, welted, with whole fronts, and Michael has made soft slippers with single soles, and has wasted the leather. What am I to say to the gentleman? I can never replace leather such as this."

And he said to Michael, "What are you doing, friend? You have ruined me! You know the gentleman ordered high boots, but see what you have made!"

Hardly had he begun to rebuke Michael when "rat-tat" went the iron ring that hung at the door. Some one was knock-

34

ing. They looked out of the window; a man had come on horseback and was fastening his horse. They opened the door, and the servant who had been with the gentleman came in.

"Good day," said he.

"Good day," replied Simon. "What can we do for you?"

"My mistress has sent me about the boots."

"What about the boots?"

"Why, my master no longer needs them. He is dead."

"Is it possible?"

"He did not live to get home after leaving you, but died in the carriage. When we reached home and the servants came to help him alight, he rolled over like a sack. He was dead already, and so stiff that he could hardly be got out of the carriage. My mistress sent me here, saying: 'Tell the bootmaker that the gentleman who ordered boots of him and left the leather for them no longer needs the boots, but that he must quickly make soft slippers for the corpse. Wait till they are ready and bring them back with you.' That is why I have come."

Michael gathered up the remnants of the leather; rolled them up, took the soft slippers he had made, slapped them together, wiped them down with his apron, and handed them and the roll of leather to the servant, who took them and said: "Goodbye, masters, and good day to you!"

VIII

Another year passed, and another, and Michael was now living his sixth year with Simon. He lived as before. He went nowhere, only spoke when necessary, and had only smiled twice in all those years—once when Matrëna gave him food, and a second time when the gentleman was in their hut. Simon was more than pleased with his workman. He never now asked him

35

where he came from, and only feared lest Michael should go away.

They were all at home one day. Matrëna was putting iron pots in the oven; the children were running along the benches and looking out of the window; Simon was sewing at one window and Michael was fastening on a heel at the other.

One of the boys ran along the bench to Michael, leant on his shoulder, and looked out of the window.

"Look, Uncle Michael! There is a lady with little girls! She seems to be coming here. And one of the girls is lame."

When the boy said that, Michael dropped his work, turned to the window, and looked out into the street.

Simon was surprised. Michael never used to look out into the street, but now he pressed against the window, staring at something. Simon also looked out and saw that a well-dressed woman was really coming to his hut, leading by the hand two little girls in fur coats and woolen shawls. The girls could hardly be told one from the other, except that one of them was crippled in her left leg and walked with a limp.

The woman stepped into the porch and entered the passage. Feeling about for the entrance she found the latch, which she lifted and opened the door. She let the two girls go in first, and followed them into the hut.

"Good day, good folk!"

"Pray come in," said Simon. "What can we do for you?"

The woman sat down by the table. The two little girls pressed close to her knees, afraid of the people in the hut.

"I want leather shoes made for these two little girls, for spring."

"We can do that. We never have made such small shoes, but we can make them; either welted or turnover shoes, linen-lined. My man, Michael, is a master at the work."

Simon glanced at Michael and saw that he had left his work

36

and was sitting with his eyes fixed on the little girls. Simon was surprised. It was true the girls were pretty, with black eyes, plump, and rosy-cheeked, and they wore nice kerchiefs and fur coats, but still Simon could not understand why Michael should look at them like that—just as if he had known them before. He was puzzled, but went on talking with the woman and arranging the price. Having fixed it, he prepared the measure. The woman lifted the lame girl on to her lap and said: "Take two measures from this little girl. Make one shoe for the lame foot and three for the sound one. They both have the same-sized feet. They are twins."

Simon took the measure and, speaking of the lame girl, said: "How did it happen to her? She is such a pretty girl. Was she born so?"

"No, her mother crushed her leg."

Then Matrëna joined in. She wondered who this woman was and whose the children were, so she said: "Are not you their mother, then?"

"No, my good woman; I am neither their mother nor any relation to them. They were quite strangers to me, but I adopted them."

"They are not your children and yet you are so fond of them?"

"How can I help being fond of them? I fed them both at my own breasts. I had a child of my own, but God took him. I was not so fond of him as I now am of these."

"Then whose children are they?"

IX

The woman, having begun talking, told them the whole story.

"It is about six years since their parents died, both in one week: their father was buried on the Tuesday, and their mother

37

died on the Friday. These orphans were born three days after their father's death, and their mother did not live another day. My husband and I were then living as peasants in the village. We were neighbors of theirs, our yard being next to theirs. Their father was a lonely man, a wood-cutter in the forest. When felling trees one day they let one fall on him. It fell across his body and crushed his bowels out. They hardly got him home before his soul went to God; and that same week his wife gave birth to twins—these little girls. She was poor and alone; she had no one, young or old, with her. Alone she gave them birth, and alone she met her death.

"The next morning I went to see her, but when I entered the hut, she, poor thing, was already stark and cold. In dying she had rolled on to this child and crushed her leg. The village folk came to the hut, washed the body, laid her out, made a coffin, and buried her. They were good folk. The babies were left alone. What was to be done with them? I was the only woman there who had a baby at the time. I was nursing my first-born —eight weeks old. So I took them for a time. The peasants came together, and thought and thought what to do with them; and at last they said to me: 'For the present, Mary, you had better keep the girls, and later on we will arrange what to do for them.' So I nursed the sound one at my breast, but at first I did not feed this crippled one. I did not suppose she would live. But then I thought to myself, why should the poor innocent suffer? I pitied her and began to feed her. And so I fed my own boy and these two—the three of them—at my own breast. I was young and strong and had good food, and God gave me so much milk that at times it even overflowed. I used sometimes to feed two at a time, while the third was waiting. When one had had enough I nursed the third. And God so ordered it that these grew up, while my own was buried before he was two years old. And I had no more children, though we prospered.

38

Now my husband is working for the corn merchant at the mill. The pay is good and we are well off. But I have no children of my own, and how lonely I should be without these little girls! How can I help loving them! They are the joy of my life!"

She pressed the lame little girl to her with one hand, while with the other she wiped the tears from her cheeks.

And Matrëna sighed, and said: "The proverb is true that says, 'One may live without father or mother, but one cannot live without God.' "

So they talked together, when suddenly the whole hut was lighted up as though by summer lightning from the corner where Michael sat. They all looked towards him and saw him sitting, his hands folded on his knees, gazing upwards and smiling.

X

The woman went away with the girls. Michael rose from the bench, put down his work, and took off his apron. Then, bowing low to Simon and his wife, he said: "Farewell, masters. God has forgiven me. I ask your forgiveness, too, for anything done amiss."

And they saw that a light shone from Michael. And Simon rose, bowed down to Michael, and said: "I see, Michael, that you are no common man, and I can neither keep you nor question you. Only tell me this: how is it that when I found you and brought you home, you were gloomy, and when my wife gave you food you smiled at her and became brighter? Then when the gentleman came to order the boots, you smiled again and became brighter still? And now, when this woman brought the little girls, you smiled a third time and have become as bright as day? Tell me, Michael, why does your face shine so, and why did you smile those three times?"

And Michael answered: "Light shines from me because I

39

have been punished, but now God has pardoned me. And I smiled three times, because God sent me to learn three truths, and I have learnt them. One I learnt when your wife pitied me, and that is why I smiled the first time. The second I learnt when the rich man ordered the boots, and then I smiled again. And now, when I saw those little girls, I learnt the third and last truth, and I smiled the third time."

And Simon said, "Tell me, Michael, what did God punish you for? And what were the three truths—that I, too, may know them?"

And Michael answered: "God punished me for disobeying Him. I was an angel in heaven and disobeyed God. God sent me to fetch a woman's soul. I flew to earth, and saw a sick woman lying alone who had just given birth to twin girls. They moved feebly at their mother's side but she could not lift them to her breast. When she saw me, she understood that God had sent me for her soul, and she wept and said: 'Angel of God! My husband has just been buried, killed by a falling tree. I have neither sister, nor aunt, nor mother: no one to care for my orphans. Do not take my soul! Let me nurse my babes, feed them, and set them on their feet before I die. Children cannot live without father or mother.' And I hearkened to her. I placed one child at her breast and gave the other into her arms, and returned to the Lord in heaven. I flew to the Lord, and said: 'I could not take the soul of the mother. Her husband was killed by a tree; the woman has twins and prays that her soul may not be taken. She says: "Let me nurse and feed my children, and set them on their feet. Children cannot live without father or mother." I have not taken her soul.' And God said: 'Go—take the mother's soul, and learn three truths: Learn *What dwells in man*, *What is not given to man*, and *What men live by*. When thou hast learnt these things, thou shalt return to heaven.' So I flew again to earth and took the mother's soul. The babes

40

dropped from her breasts. Her body rolled over on the bed and crushed one babe, twisting its leg. I rose above the village, wishing to take her soul to God, but a wind seized me and my wings drooped and dropped off. Her soul rose alone to God, while I fell to earth by the roadside."

XI

And Simon and Matrëna understood who it was that had lived with them, and whom they had clothed and fed. And they wept with awe and with joy. And the angel said: "I was alone in the field, naked. I had never known human needs, cold and hunger, till I became a man. I was famished, frozen, and did not know what to do. I saw, near the field I was in, a shrine built for God, and I went to it hoping to find shelter. But the shrine was locked and I could not enter. So I sat down behind the shrine to shelter myself at least from the wind. Evening drew on, I was hungry, frozen, and in pain. Suddenly I heard a man coming along the road. He carried a pair of boots and was talking to himself. For the first time since I became a man I saw the mortal face of a man, and his face seemed terrible to me and I turned from it. And I heard the man talking to himself of how to cover his body from the cold in winter, and how to feed wife and children. And I thought: 'I am perishing of cold and hunger and here is a man thinking only of how to clothe himself and his wife, and how to get bread for themselves. He cannot help me.' When the man saw me he frowned and became still more terrible, and passed me by on the other side. I despaired; but suddenly I heard him coming back. I looked up and did not recognize the same man: before, I had seen death in his face; but now he was alive and I recognized in him the presence of God. He came up to me, clothed me, took me with him, and brought me to his home. I entered the house; a

41

woman came to meet us and began to speak. The woman was still more terrible than the man had been; the spirit of death came from her mouth; I could not breathe for the stench of death that spread around her. She wished to drive me out into the cold, and I knew that if she did so she would die. Suddenly her husband spoke to her of God, and the woman changed at once. And when she brought me food and looked at me, I glanced at her and saw that death no longer dwelt in her; she had become alive, and in her too I saw God.

"Then I remembered the first lesson God had set me: '*Learn what dwells in man.*' And I understood that in man dwells Love! I was glad that God had already begun to show me what He had promised, and I smiled for the first time. But I had not yet learnt all. I did not yet know *What is not given to man*, and *What men live by.*

"I lived with you and a year passed. A man came to order boots that should wear for a year without losing shape or cracking. I looked at him, and suddenly, behind his shoulder, I saw my comrade—the angel of death. None but me saw that angel; but I knew him, and knew that before the sun set he would take that rich man's soul. And I thought to myself, 'The man is making preparations for a year and does not know that he will die before evening.' And I remembered God's second saying, '*Learn what is not given to man.*'

"What dwells in man I already knew. Now I learnt what is not given him. It is not given to man to know his own needs. And I smiled for the second time. I was glad to have seen my comrade angel—glad also that God had revealed to me the second saying.

"But I still did not know all. I did not know *What men live by.* And I lived on, waiting till God should reveal to me the last lesson. In the sixth year came the girl-twins with the woman; and I recognized the girls and heard how they had been kept

42

alive. Having heard the story, I thought, 'Their mother besought me for the children's sake, and I believed her when she said that children cannot live without father or mother; but a stranger has nursed them, and has brought them up.' And when the woman showed her love for the children that were not her own, and wept over them, I saw in her the living God, and understood *What men live by*. And I knew that God had revealed to me the last lesson, and had forgiven my sin. And then I smiled for the third time."

XII

And the angel's body was bared, and he was clothed in light so that eye could not look on him; and his voice grew louder, as though it came not from him but from heaven above. And the angel said:

"I have learnt that all men live not by care for themselves, but by love.

"It was not given to the mother to know what her children needed for their life. Nor was it given to the rich man to know what he himself needed. Nor is it given to any man to know whether, when evening comes, he will need boots for his body or slippers for his corpse.

"I remained alive when I was a man, not by care of myself but because love was present in a passer-by, and because he and his wife pitied and loved me. The orphans remained alive not because of their mother's care, but because there was love in the heart of a woman, a stranger to them, who pitied and loved them. And all men live not by the thought they spend on their own welfare, but because love exists in man.

"I knew before that God gave life to men and desires that they should live; now I understood more than that.

"I understood that God does not wish men to live apart, and

therefore he does not reveal to them what each one needs for himself; but he wishes them to live united, and therefore reveals to each of them what is necessary for all.

"I have now understood that though it seems to men that they live by care for themselves, in truth it is love alone by which they live. He who has love, is in God, and God is in him, for God is love."

And the angel sang praise to God, so that the hut trembled at his voice. The roof opened, and a column of fire rose from earth to heaven. Simon and his wife and children fell to the ground. Wings appeared upon the angel's shoulders and he rose into the heavens.

And when Simon came to himself the hut stood as before, and there was no one in it but his own family.

1881.

How Much Land Does a Man Need?

AN elder sister came to visit her younger sister in the country. The elder was married to a tradesman in town, the
younger to a peasant in the village. As the sisters sat over their
tea talking, the elder began to boast of the advantages of town

life: saying how comfortably they lived there, how well they dressed, what fine clothes her children wore, what good things they ate and drank, and how she went to the theatre, promenades, and entertainments.

The younger sister was piqued, and in turn disparaged the life of a tradesman, and stood up for that of a peasant.

"I would not change my way of life for yours," said she. "We may live roughly, but at least we are free from anxiety. You live in better style than we do, but though you often earn more than you need, you are very likely to lose all you have. You know the proverb, 'Loss and gain are brothers twain.' It often happens that people who are wealthy one day are begging their bread the next. Our way is safer. Though a peasant's life is not a fat one, it is a long one. We shall never grow rich, but we shall always have enough to eat."

The elder sister said sneeringly:

"Enough? Yes, if you like to share with the pigs and the calves! What do you know of elegance or manners! However much your goodman may slave, you will die as you are living—on a dung heap—and your children the same."

"Well, what of that?" replied the younger. "Of course our work is rough and coarse. But, on the other hand, it is sure, and we need not bow to anyone. But you, in your towns, are surrounded by temptations; to-day all may be right, but to-morrow the Evil One may tempt your husband with cards, wine, or women, and all will go to ruin. Don't such things happen often enough?"

Pahóm, the master of the house, was lying on the top of the stove and he listened to the women's chatter.

"It is perfectly true," thought he. "Busy as we are from childhood tilling mother earth, we peasants have no time to let any nonsense settle in our heads. Our only trouble is that we

48

haven't land enough. If I had plenty of land, I shouldn't fear the Devil himself!"

The women finished their tea, chatted a while about dress, and then cleared away the tea-things and lay down to sleep.

But the Devil had been sitting behind the stove, and had heard all that was said. He was pleased that the peasant's wife had led her husband into boasting, and that he had said that if he had plenty of land he would not fear the Devil himself.

"All right," thought the Devil. "We will have a tussle. I'll give you land enough; and by means of that land I will get you into my power."

II

Close to the village there lived a lady, a small landowner who had an estate of about three hundred acres.[1] She had always lived on good terms with the peasants until she engaged as her steward an old soldier, who took to burdening the people with fines. However careful Pahóm tried to be, it happened again and again that now a horse of his got among the lady's oats, now a cow strayed into her garden, now his calves found their way into her meadows—and he always had to pay a fine.

Pahóm paid up, but grumbled and, going home in a temper, was rough with his family. All through that summer, Pahóm had much trouble because of this steward, and he was even glad when winter came and the cattle had to be stabled. Though he grudged the fodder when they could no longer graze on the pasture-land, at least he was free from anxiety about them.

In the winter the news got about that the lady was going to sell her land and that the keeper of the inn on the high road was bargaining for it. When the peasants heard this they were very much alarmed.

[1] 120 desyatíns. The desyatína is properly 2.7 acres; but in this story round numbers are used.

49

"Well," thought they, "if the innkeeper gets the land, he will worry us with fines worse than the lady's steward. We all depend on that estate."

So the peasants went on behalf of their Commune, and asked the lady not to sell the land to the innkeeper, offering her a better price for it themselves. The lady agreed to let them have it. Then the peasants tried to arrange for the Commune to buy the whole estate, so that it might be held by them all in common. They met twice to discuss it, but could not settle the matter; the Evil One sowed discord among them and they could not agree. So they decided to buy the land individually, each according to his means; and the lady agreed to this plan as she had to the other.

Presently Pahóm heard that a neighbor of his was buying fifty acres, and that the lady had consented to accept one half in cash and to wait a year for the other half. Pahóm felt envious.

"Look at that," thought he, "the land is all being sold, and I shall get none of it." So he spoke to his wife.

"Other people are buying," said he, "and we must also buy twenty acres or so. Life is becoming impossible. That steward is simply crushing us with his fines."

So they put their heads together and considered how they could manage to buy it. They had one hundred rúbles laid by. They sold a colt and one half of their bees, hired out one of their sons as a laborer and took his wages in advance; borrowed the rest from a brother-in-law, and so scraped together half the purchase money.

Having done this, Pahóm chose out a farm of forty acres, some of it wooded, and went to the lady to bargain for it. They came to an agreement, and he shook hands with her upon it and paid her a deposit in advance. Then they went to town and signed the deeds; he paying half the price down, and undertaking to pay the remainder within two years.

50

So now Pahóm had land of his own. He borrowed seed, and sowed it on the land he had bought. The harvest was a good one, and within a year he had managed to pay off his debts both to the lady and to his brother-in-law. So he became a landowner, ploughing and sowing his own land, making hay on his own land, cutting his own trees, and feeding his cattle on his own pasture. When he went out to plough his fields, or to look at his growing corn, or at his grass-meadows, his heart would fill with joy. The grass that grew and the flowers that bloomed there seemed to him unlike any that grew elsewhere. Formerly, when he had passed by that land, it had appeared the same as any other land, but now it seemed quite different.

III

So Pahóm was well-contented, and everything would have been right if the neighboring peasants would only not have trespassed on his corn-fields and meadows. He appealed to them most civilly, but they still went on: now the Communal herdsmen would let the village cows stray into his meadows, then horses from the night pasture would get among his corn. Pahóm turned them out again and again, and forgave their owners, and for a long time he forbore to prosecute any one. But at last he lost patience and complained to the District Court. He knew it was the peasants' want of land, and no evil intent on their part, that caused the trouble, but he thought:

"I cannot go on overlooking it or they will destroy all I have. They must be taught a lesson."

So he had them up, gave them one lesson, and then another, and two or three of the peasants were fined. After a time Pahóm's neighbors began to bear him a grudge for this, and would now and then let their cattle on to his land on purpose. One peasant even got into Pahóm's wood at night and cut down five young lime trees for their bark. Pahóm passing through the wood one day noticed something white. He came nearer and saw the stripped trunks lying on the ground, and close by stood the stumps where the trees had been. Pahóm was furious.

"If he had only cut one here and there it would have been bad enough," thought Pahóm, "but the rascal has actually cut down a whole clump. If I could only find out who did this, I would pay him out."

He racked his brain as to who it could be. Finally he decided: "It must be Simon—no one else could have done it." So he went to Simon's homestead to have a look round, but he found nothing, and only had an angry scene. However, he now felt more certain than ever that Simon had done it, and he lodged a complaint. Simon was summoned. The case was tried, and retried, and at the end of it all Simon was acquitted, there being no evidence against him. Pahóm felt still more aggrieved, and let his anger loose upon the Elder and the Judges.

"You let thieves grease your palms," said he. "If you were honest folk yourselves you would not let a thief go free."

So Pahóm quarrelled with the Judges and with his neighbors. Threats to burn his building began to be uttered. So though Pahóm had more land, his place in the Commune was much worse than before.

About this time a rumor got about that many people were moving to new parts.

"There's no need for me to leave my land," thought Pahóm. "But some of the others might leave our village and then there would be more room for us. I would take over their land myself and make my estate a bit bigger. I could then live more at ease. As it is, I am still too cramped to be comfortable."

One day Pahóm was sitting at home when a peasant, passing through the village, happened to call in. He was allowed to stay the night, and supper was given him. Pahóm had a talk

52

with this peasant and asked him where he came from. The stranger answered that he came from beyond the Vólga, where he had been working. One word led to another, and the man went on to say that many people were settling in those parts. He told how some people from his village had settled there. They had joined the Commune, and had had twenty-five acres per man granted them. The land was so good, he said, that the rye sown on it grew as high as a horse, and so thick that five cuts of a sickle made a sheaf. One peasant, he said, had brought nothing with him but his bare hands, and now he had six horses and two cows of his own.

Pahóm's heart kindled with desire. He thought:

"Why should I suffer in this narrow hole, if one can live so well elsewhere? I will sell my land and my homestead here, and with the money I will start afresh over there and get everything new. In this crowded place one is always having trouble. But I must first go and find out all about it myself."

Towards summer he got ready and started. He went down the Vólga on a steamer to Samára, then walked another three hundred miles on foot, and at last reached the place. It was just as the stranger had said. The peasants had plenty of land: every man had twenty-five acres of Communal land given him for his use, and any one who had money could buy, besides, at a rúble an acre as much good freehold land as he wanted.

Having found out all he wished to know, Pahóm returned home as autumn came on, and began selling off his belongings. He sold his land at a profit, sold his homestead and all his cattle, and withdrew from membership in the Commune. He only waited till the spring, and then started with his family for the new settlement.

IV

As soon as Pahóm and his family reached their new abode, he applied for admission into the Commune of a large village. He stood treat to the Elders and obtained the necessary documents. Five shares of Communal land were given him for his own and his sons' use: that is to say—125 acres (not all together, but in different fields) besides the use of the Communal pasture. Pahóm put up the buildings he needed, and bought cattle. Of the Communal land alone he had three times as much as at his former home, and the land was good corn-land. He was ten times better off than he had been. He had plenty of arable land and pasturage, and could keep as many head of cattle as he liked.

At first, in the bustle of building and settling down, Pahóm was pleased with it all, but when he got used to it he began to think that even here he had not enough land. The first year, he sowed wheat on his share of the Communal land and had a good crop. He wanted to go on sowing wheat, but had not enough Communal land for the purpose, and what he had already used was not available; for in those parts wheat is only sown on virgin soil or on fallow land. It is sown for one or two years, and then the land lies fallow till it is again overgrown with prairie grass. There were many who wanted such land and there was not enough for all; so that people quarreled about it. Those who were better off wanted it for growing wheat, and those who were poor wanted it to let to dealers, so that they might raise money to pay their taxes. Pahóm wanted to sow more wheat, so he rented land from a dealer for a year. He sowed much wheat and had a fine crop, but the land was too far from the village—the wheat had to be carted more than ten miles. After a time Pahóm noticed that some peasant-dealers

54

were living on separate farms and were growing wealthy; and he thought:

"If I were to buy some freehold land and have a homestead on it, it would be a different thing altogether. Then it would all be nice and compact."

The question of buying freehold land recurred to him again and again.

He went on in the same way for three years, renting land and sowing wheat. The seasons turned out well and the crops were good, so that he began to lay money by. He might have gone on living contentedly, but he grew tired of having to rent other people's land every year, and having to scramble for it. Wherever there was good land to be had, the peasants would rush for it and it was taken up at once, so that unless you were sharp about it you got none. It happened in the third year that he and a dealer together rented a piece of pasture-land from some peasants; and they had already ploughed it up, when there was some dispute and the peasants went to law about it, and things fell out so that the labor was all lost.

"If it were my own land," thought Pahóm, "I should be independent, and there would not be all this unpleasantness."

So Pahóm began looking out for land which he could buy; and he came across a peasant who had bought thirteen hundred acres, but having got into difficulties was willing to sell again cheap. Pahóm bargained and haggled with him, and at last they settled the price at 1,500 rúbles, part in cash and part to be paid later. They had all but clinched the matter when a passing dealer happened to stop at Pahóm's one day to get a feed for his horses. He drank tea with Pahóm and they had a talk. The dealer said that he was just returning from the land of the Bash-kírs, far away, where he had bought thirteen thousand acres of land, all for 1,000 rúbles. Pahóm questioned him further, and the tradesman said:

"All one need do is to make friends with the chiefs. I gave away about one hundred rúbles' worth of silk robes and carpets, besides a case of tea, and I gave wine to those who would drink it; and I got the land for less than a penny an acre." [1] And he showed Pahóm the title-deeds, saying:

"The land lies near a river, and the whole prairie is virgin soil."

Pahóm plied him with questions, and the tradesman said:

"There is more land there than you could cover if you walked a year, and it all belongs to the Bashkírs. They are as simple as sheep, and land can be got almost for nothing."

"There now," thought Pahóm, "with my one thousand rúbles, why should I get only thirteen hundred acres, and saddle myself with a debt besides? If I take it out there, I can get more than ten times as much for the money."

V

Pahóm inquired how to get to the place, and as soon as the tradesman had left him, he prepared to go there himself. He left his wife to look after the homestead, and started on his journey taking his man with him. They stopped at a town on their way and bought a case of tea, some wine, and other presents, as the tradesman had advised. On and on they went until they had gone more than three hundred miles, and on the seventh day they came to a place where the Bashkírs had pitched their tents. It was all just as the tradesman had said. The people lived on the steppes, by a river, in felt-covered tents.[2] They neither tilled the ground, nor ate bread. Their cattle and horses grazed in herds on the steppe. The colts were tethered behind the tents, and the mares were driven to them twice a day. The

---

[1] Five kopéks for a desyatína. [2] A kibítka is a movable dwelling, made up of detachable wooden frames, forming a round, and covered over with felt.

mares were milked, and from the milk kumiss was made. It was the women who prepared kumiss, and they also made cheese. As far as the men were concerned, drinking kumiss and tea, eating mutton, and playing on their pipes, was all they cared about. They were all stout and merry, and all the summer long they never thought of doing any work. They were quite ignorant, and knew no Russian, but were good-natured enough.

As soon as they saw Pahóm, they came out of their tents and gathered round their visitor. An interpreter was found, and Pahóm told them he had come about some land. The Bashkírs seemed very glad; they took Pahóm and led him into one of the best tents, where they made him sit on some down cushions placed on a carpet, while they sat round him. They gave him some tea and kumiss, and had a sheep killed, and gave him mutton to eat. Pahóm took presents out of his cart and distributed them among the Bashkírs, and divided the tea amongst them. The Bashkírs were delighted. They talked a great deal among themselves, and then told the interpreter to translate.

"They wish to tell you," said the interpreter, "that they like you, and that it is our custom to do all we can to please a guest and to repay him for his gifts. You have given us presents, now tell us which of the things we possess please you best, that we may present them to you."

"What pleases me best here," answered Pahóm, "is your land. Our land is crowded and the soil is exhausted; but you have plenty of land and it is good land. I never saw the like of it."

The interpreter translated. The Bashkírs talked among themselves for a while. Pahóm could not understand what they were saying, but saw that they were much amused and that they shouted and laughed. Then they were silent and looked at Pahóm while the interpreter said:

"They wish me to tell you that in return for your presents

they will gladly give you as much land as you want. You have only to point it out with your hand and it is yours."

The Bashkírs talked again for a while and began to dispute. Pahóm asked what they were disputing about, and the interpreter told him that some of them thought they ought to ask their Chief about the land and not act in his absence, while others thought there was no need to wait for his return.

VI

While the Bashkírs were disputing, a man in a large fox-fur cap appeared on the scene. They all became silent and rose to their feet. The interpreter said, "This is our Chief himself."

Pahóm immediately fetched the best dressing-gown and five pounds of tea, and offered these to the Chief. The Chief accepted them, and seated himself in the place of honor. The Bashkírs at once began telling him something. The Chief listened for a while, then made a sign with his head for them to be silent, and addressing himself to Pahóm, said in Russian:

"Well, let it be so. Choose whatever piece of land you like; we have plenty of it."

"How can I take as much as I like?" thought Pahóm. "I must get a deed to make it secure, or else they may say, 'It is yours,' and afterwards may take it away again."

"Thank you for your kind words," he said aloud. "You have much land, and I only want a little. But I should like to be sure which bit is mine. Could it not be measured and made over to me? Life and death are in God's hands. You good people give it to me, but your children might wish to take it away again."

"You are quite right," said the Chief. "We will make it over to you."

"I heard that a dealer had been here," continued Pahóm,
58

"and that you gave him a little land, too, and signed title-deeds to that effect. I should like to have it done in the same way."

The Chief understood.

"Yes," replied he, "that can be done quite easily. We have a scribe, and we will go to town with you and have the deed properly sealed."

"And what will be the price?" asked Pahóm.

"Our price is always the same: one thousand rúbles a day."

Pahóm did not understand.

"A day? What measure is that? How many acres would that be?"

"We do not know how to reckon it out," said the Chief. "We sell it by the day. As much as you can go round on your feet in a day is yours, and the price is one thousand rúbles a day."

Pahóm was surprised.

"But in a day you can get round a large tract of land," he said.

The Chief laughed.

"It will all be yours!" said he. "But there is one condition: If you don't return on the same day to the spot whence you started, your money is lost."

"But how am I to mark the way that I have gone?"

"Why, we shall go to any spot you like, and stay there. You must start from that spot and make your round, taking a spade with you. Wherever you think necessary, make a mark. At every turning, dig a hole and pile up the turf; then afterwards we will go round with a plough from hole to hole. You may make as large a circuit as you please, but before the sun sets you must return to the place you started from. All the land you cover will be yours."

Pahóm was delighted. It was decided to start early next morning. They talked a while, and after drinking some more kumiss and eating some more mutton, they had tea again, and then

59

the night came on. They gave Pahóm a feather-bed to sleep on, and the Bashkírs dispersed for the night, promising to assemble the next morning at daybreak and ride out before sunrise to the appointed spot.

VII

Pahóm lay on the feather-bed, but could not sleep. He kept thinking about the land.

"What a large tract I will mark off!" thought he. "I can easily do thirty-five miles in a day. The days are long now, and within a circuit of thirty-five miles what a lot of land there will be! I will sell the poorer land, or let it to peasants, but I'll pick out the best and farm it. I will buy two oxteams, and hire two more laborers. About a hundred and fifty acres shall be plough-land, and I will pasture cattle on the rest."

Pahóm lay awake all night, and dozed off only just before dawn. Hardly were his eyes closed when he had a dream. He thought he was lying in that same tent and heard somebody chuckling outside. He wondered who it could be, and rose and went out, and he saw the Bashkír Chief sitting in front of the tent holding his sides and rolling about with laughter. Going nearer to the Chief, Pahóm asked: "What are you laughing at?" But he saw that it was no longer the Chief, but the dealer who had recently stopped at his house and had told him about the land. Just as Pahóm was going to ask, "Have you been here long?" he saw that it was not the dealer, but the peasant who had come up from the Vólga, long ago, to Pahóm's old home. Then he saw that it was not the peasant either, but the Devil himself with hoofs and horns, sitting there and chuckling, and before him lay a man barefoot, prostrate on the ground, with only trousers and a shirt on. And Pahóm dreamt that he looked more attentively to see what sort of a man it was that was lying

60

there, and he saw that the man was dead, and that it was himself! He awoke horror-struck.

"What things one does dream," thought he.

Looking round he saw through the open door that the dawn was breaking.

"It's time to wake them up," thought he. "We ought to be starting."

He got up, roused his man (who was sleeping in his cart), bade him harness; and went to call the Bashkírs.

"It's time to go to the steppe to measure the land," he said.

The Bashkírs rose and assembled, and the Chief came too. Then they began drinking kumiss again, and offered Pahóm some tea, but he would not wait.

"If we are to go, let us go. It is high time," said he.

VIII

The Bashkírs got ready and they all started: some mounted on horses, and some in carts. Pahóm drove in his own small cart with his servant and took a spade with him. When they reached the steppe, the morning red was beginning to kindle. They ascended a hillock (called by the Bashkírs a *shikhan*) and dismounting from their carts and their horses, gathered in one spot. The Chief came up to Pahóm and stretching out his arm towards the plain:

"See," said he, "all this, as far as your eye can reach, is ours. You may have any part of it you like."

Pahóm's eyes glistened: it was all virgin soil, as flat as the palm of your hand, as black as the seed of a poppy, and in the hollows different kinds of grasses grew breast high.

The Chief took off his fox-fur cap, placed it on the ground and said:

61

"This will be the mark. Start from here, and return here again. All the land you go round shall be yours."

Pahóm took out his money and put it on the cap. Then he took off his outer coat, remaining in his sleeveless under-coat. He unfastened his girdle and tied it tight below his stomach, put a little bag of bread into the breast of his coat, and tying a flask of water to his girdle, he drew up the tops of his boots, took the spade from his man, and stood ready to start. He considered for some moments which way he had better go—it was tempting everywhere.

"No matter," he concluded, "I will go towards the rising sun."

He turned his face to the east, stretched himself, and waited for the sun to appear above the rim.

"I must lose no time," he thought, "and it is easier walking while it is still cool."

The sun's rays had hardly flashed above the horizon, before Pahóm, carrying the spade over his shoulder, went down into the steppe.

Pahóm started walking neither slowly nor quickly. After having gone a thousand yards he stopped, dug a hole, and placed pieces of turf one on another to make it more visible. Then he went on; and now that he had walked off his stiffness he quickened his pace. After a while he dug another hole.

Pahóm looked back. The hillock could be distinctly seen in the sunlight, with the people on it, and the glittering tires of the cart-wheels. At a rough guess Pahóm concluded that he had walked three miles. It was growing warmer; he took off his under-coat, flung it across his shoulder, and went on again. It had grown quite warm now; he looked at the sun, it was time to think of breakfast.

"The first shift is done, but there are four in a day, and it is too soon yet to turn. But I will just take off my boots," said he to himself.

He sat down, took off his boots, stuck them into his girdle, and went on. It was easy walking now.

"I will go on for another three miles," thought he, "and then turn to the left. This spot is so fine, that it would be a pity to lose it. The further one goes, the better the land seems."

He went straight on for a while, and when he looked round, the hillock was scarcely visible and the people on it looked like black ants, and he could just see something glistening there in the sun.

"Ah," thought Pahóm, "I have gone far enough in this direction, it is time to turn. Besides I am in a regular sweat, and very thirsty."

He stopped, dug a large hole, and heaped up pieces of turf. Next he untied his flask, had a drink, and then turned sharply to the left. He went on and on; the grass was high, and it was very hot.

Pahóm began to grow tired: he looked at the sun and saw that it was noon.

"Well," he thought, "I must have a rest."

He sat down, and ate some bread and drank some water; but he did not lie down, thinking that if he did he might fall asleep. After sitting a little while, he went on again. At first he walked easily: the food had strengthened him; but it had become terribly hot and he felt sleepy, still he went on, thinking: "An hour to suffer, a life-time to live."

He went a long way in this direction also, and was about to turn to the left again, when he perceived a damp hollow: "It would be a pity to leave that out," he thought. "Flax would do well there." So he went on past the hollow, and dug a hole on the other side of it before he turned the corner. Pahóm looked towards the hillock. The heat made the air hazy: it seemed to

63

be quivering, and through the haze the people on the hillock could scarcely be seen.

"Ah!" thought Pahóm, "I have made the sides too long; I must make this one shorter." And he went along the third side, stepping faster. He looked at the sun: it was nearly half-way to the horizon, and he had not yet done two miles of the third side of the square. He was still ten miles from the goal.

"No," he thought, "though it will make my land lop-sided, I must hurry back in a straight line now. I might go too far, and as it is I have a great deal of land."

So Pahóm hurriedly dug a hole, and turned straight towards the hillock.

IX

Pahóm went straight towards the hillock, but he now walked with difficulty. He was done up with the heat, his bare feet were cut and bruised, and his legs began to fail. He longed to rest, but it was impossible if he meant to get back before sunset. The sun waits for no man, and it was sinking lower and lower.

"Oh dear," he thought, "if only I have not blundered trying for too much! What if I am too late?"

He looked towards the hillock and at the sun. He was still far from his goal, and the sun was already near the rim.

Pahóm walked on and on; it was very hard walking but he went quicker and quicker. He pressed on, but was still far from the place. He began running, threw away his coat, his boots, his flask, and his cap, and kept only the spade which he used as a support.

"What shall I do," he thought again, "I have grasped too much and ruined the whole affair. I can't get there before the sun sets."

And this fear made him still more breathless. Pahóm went on running, his soaking shirt and trousers stuck to him and his

64

mouth was parched. His breast was working like a blacksmith's bellows, his heart was beating like a hammer, and his legs were giving way as if they did not belong to him. Pahóm was seized with terror lest he should die of the strain.

Though afraid of death, he could not stop. "After having run all that way they will call me a fool if I stop now," thought he. And he ran on and on, and drew near and heard the Bashkírs yelling and shouting to him, and their cries inflamed his heart still more. He gathered his last strength and ran on.

The sun was close to the rim, and cloaked in mist looked large, and red as blood. Now, yes now, it was about to set! The sun was quite low, but he was also quite near his aim. Pahóm could already see the people on the hillock waving their arms to hurry him up. He could see the fox-fur cap on the ground and the money on it, and the Chief sitting on the ground holding his sides. And Pahóm remembered his dream.

"There is plenty of land," thought he, "but will God let me live on it? I have lost my life, I have lost my life! I shall never reach that spot!"

Pahóm looked at the sun, which had reached the earth: one side of it had already disappeared. With all his remaining strength he rushed on, bending his body forward so that his legs could hardly follow fast enough to keep him from falling. Just as he reached the hillock it suddenly grew dark. He looked up—the sun had already set! He gave a cry: "All my labor has been in vain," thought he, and was about to stop, but he heard the Bashkírs still shouting, and remembered that though to him, from below, the sun seemed to have set, they on the hillock could still see it. He took a long breath and ran up the hillock. It was still light there. He reached the top and saw the cap. Before it sat the Chief laughing and holding his sides. Again Pahóm remembered his dream, and he uttered a cry: his legs

65

gave way beneath him, he fell forward and reached the cap with his hands.

"Ah, that's a fine fellow!" exclaimed the Chief. "He has gained much land!"

Pahóm's servant came running up and tried to raise him, but he saw that blood was flowing from his mouth. Pahóm was dead!

The Bashkírs clicked their tongues to show their pity.

His servant picked up the spade and dug a grave long enough for Pahóm to lie in, and buried him in it. Six feet from his head to his heels was all he needed.

1886.

The Three Hermits

An Old Legend Current in the Vólga District

A BISHOP was sailing from Archangel to the Solovétsk
Monastery, and on the same vessel were a number of
pilgrims on their way to visit the shrines at that place. The
voyage was a smooth one. The wind favorable and the weather

fair. The pilgrims lay on deck, eating, or sat in groups talking to one another. The Bishop, too, came on deck, and as he was pacing up and down he noticed a group of men standing near the prow and listening to a fisherman, who was pointing to the sea and telling them something. The Bishop stopped, and looked in the direction in which the man was pointing. He could see nothing, however, but the sea glistening in the sunshine. He drew nearer to listen, but when the man saw him, he took off his cap and was silent. The rest of the people also took off their caps and bowed.

"Do not let me disturb you, friends," said the Bishop. "I came to hear what this good man was saying."

"The fisherman was telling us about the hermits," replied one, a tradesman, rather bolder than the rest.

"What hermits?" asked the Bishop, going to the side of the vessel and seating himself on a box. "Tell me about them. I should like to hear. What were you pointing at?"

"Why, that little island you can just see over there," answered the man, pointing to a spot ahead and a little to the right. "That is the island where the hermits live for the salvation of their souls."

"Where is the island?" asked the Bishop. "I see nothing."

"There, in the distance, if you will please look along my hand. Do you see that little cloud? Below it, and a bit to the left, there is just a faint streak. That is the island."

The Bishop looked carefully, but his unaccustomed eyes could make out nothing but the water shimmering in the sun.

"I cannot see it," he said. "But who are the hermits that live there?"

"They are holy men," answered the fisherman. "I had long heard tell of them, but never chanced to see them myself till the year before last."

And the fisherman related how once, when he was out fish-

70

ing, he had been stranded at night upon that island, not knowing where he was. In the morning, as he wandered about the island, he came across an earth hut, and met an old man standing near it. Presently two others came out, and after having fed him and dried his things, they helped him mend his boat.

"And what are they like?" asked the Bishop.

"One is a small man and his back is bent. He wears a priest's cassock and is very old; he must be more than a hundred, I should say. He is so old that the white of his beard is taking a greenish tinge, but he is always smiling, and his face is as bright as an angel's from heaven. The second is taller, but he also is very old. He wears a tattered peasant coat. His beard is broad, and of a yellowish grey color. He is a strong man. Before I had time to help him, he turned my boat over as if it were only a pail. He too is kindly and cheerful. The third is tall, and has a beard as white as snow and reaching to his knees. He is stern, with overhanging eyebrows; and he wears nothing but a piece of matting tied round his waist."

"And did they speak to you?" asked the Bishop.

"For the most part they did everything in silence, and spoke but little even to one another. One of them would just give a glance, and the others would understand him. I asked the tallest whether they had lived there long. He frowned, and muttered something as if he were angry; but the oldest one took his hand and smiled, and then the tall one was quiet. The oldest one only said: 'Have mercy upon us,' and smiled."

While the fisherman was talking, the ship had drawn nearer to the island.

"There, now you can see it plainly, if your Lordship will please to look," said the tradesman, pointing with his hand.

The Bishop looked, and now he really saw a dark streak—which was the island. Having looked at it a while, he left the prow of the vessel, and going to the stern, asked the helmsman:

71

"What island is that?"

"That one," replied the man, "has no name. There are many such in this sea."

"Is it true that there are hermits who live there for the salvation of their souls?"

"So it is said, your Lordship, but I don't know if it's true. Fishermen say they have seen them; but of course they may only be spinning yarns."

"I should like to land on the island and see these men," said the Bishop. "How could I manage it?"

"The ship cannot get close to the island," replied the helmsman, "but you might be rowed there in a boat. You had better speak to the captain."

The captain was sent for and came.

"I should like to see these hermits," said the Bishop. "Could I not be rowed ashore?"

The captain tried to dissuade him.

"Of course it could be done," said he, "but we should lose much time. And if I might venture to say so to your Lordship, the old men are not worth your pains. I have heard say that they are foolish old fellows, who understand nothing, and never speak a word, any more than the fish in the sea."

"I wish to see them," said the Bishop, "and I will pay you for your trouble and loss of time. Please let me have a boat."

There was no help for it; so the order was given. The sailors trimmed the sails, the steersman put up the helm, and the ship's course was set for the island. A chair was placed at the prow for the Bishop, and he sat there, looking ahead. The passengers all collected at the prow, and gazed at the island. Those who had the sharpest eyes could presently make out the rocks on it, and then a mud hut was seen. At last one man saw the hermits themselves. The captain brought a telescope and, after looking through it, handed it to the Bishop.

72

"It's right enough. There are three men standing on the shore. There, a little to the right of that big rock."

The Bishop took the telescope, got it into position, and he saw the three men: a tall one, a shorter one, and one very small and bent, standing on the shore and holding each other by the hand.

The captain turned to the Bishop.

"The vessel can get no nearer in than this, your Lordship. If you wish to go ashore, we must ask you to go in the boat, while we anchor here."

The cable was quickly let out; the anchor cast, and the sails furled. There was a jerk, and the vessel shook. Then, a boat having been lowered, the oarsmen jumped in, and the Bishop descended the ladder and took his seat. The men pulled at their oars and the boat moved rapidly towards the island. When they came within a stone's throw, they saw three old men: a tall one with only a piece of matting tied round his waist: a shorter one in a tattered peasant coat, and a very old one bent with age and wearing an old cassock—all three standing hand in hand.

The oarsmen pulled in to the shore, and held on with the boathook while the Bishop got out.

The old men bowed to him, and he gave them his blessing, at which they bowed still lower. Then the Bishop began to speak to them.

"I have heard," he said, "that you, godly men, live here saving your own souls and praying to our Lord Christ for your fellow men. I, an unworthy servant of Christ, am called, by God's mercy, to keep and teach His flock. I wished to see you, servants of God, and to do what I can to teach you, also."

The old men looked at each other smiling, but remained silent.

"Tell me," said the Bishop, "what you are doing to save your souls, and how you serve God on this island."

73

The second hermit sighed, and looked at the oldest, the very ancient one. The latter smiled, and said:

"We do not know how to serve God. We only serve and support ourselves, servant of God."

"But how do you pray to God?" asked the Bishop.

"We pray in this way," replied the hermit. "Three are ye, three are we, have mercy upon us."

And when the old man said this, all three raised their eyes to heaven, and repeated:

"Three are ye, three are we, have mercy upon us!"

The Bishop smiled.

"You have evidently heard something about the Holy Trinity," said he. "But you do not pray aright. You have won my affection, godly men. I see you wish to please the Lord, but you do not know how to serve Him. That is not the way to pray; but listen to me, and I will teach you. I will teach you, not a way of my own, but the way in which God in the Holy Scriptures has commanded all men to pray to Him."

And the Bishop began explaining to the hermits how God had revealed Himself to men; telling them of God the Father, and God the Son, and God the Holy Ghost.

"God the Son came down on earth," said he, "to save men, and this is how He taught us all to pray. Listen, and repeat after me: 'Our Father.'"

And the first old man repeated after him, "Our Father," and the second said, "Our Father," and the third said, "Our Father."

"Which art in heaven," continued the Bishop.

The first hermit repeated, "Which art in heaven," but the second blundered over the words, and the tall hermit could not say them properly. His hair had grown over his mouth so that he could not speak plainly. The very old hermit, having no teeth, also mumbled indistinctly.

74

The Bishop repeated the words again, and the old men repeated them after him. The Bishop sat down on a stone, and the old men stood before him, watching his mouth, and repeating the words as he uttered them. And all day long the Bishop labored, saying a word twenty, thirty, a hundred times over, and the old men repeated it after him. They blundered, and he corrected them, and made them begin again.

The Bishop did not leave off till he had taught them the whole of the Lord's Prayer so that they could not only repeat it after him, but could say it by themselves. The middle one was the first to know it, and to repeat the whole of it alone. The Bishop made him say it again and again, and at last the others could say it too.

It was getting dark and the moon was appearing over the water, before the Bishop rose to return to the vessel. When he took leave of the old men they all bowed down to the ground before him. He raised them, and kissed each of them, telling them to pray as he had taught them. Then he got into the boat and returned to the ship.

And as he sat in the boat and was rowed to the ship he could hear the three voices of the hermits loudly repeating the Lord's Prayer. As the boat drew near the vessel their voices could no longer be heard, but they could still be seen in the moonlight, standing as he had left them on the shore, the shortest in the middle, the tallest on the right, the middle one on the left. As soon as the Bishop had reached the vessel and got on board, the anchor was weighed and the sails unfurled. The wind filled them and the ship sailed away, and the Bishop took a seat in the stern and watched the island they had left. For a time he could still see the hermits, but presently they disappeared from sight, though the island was still visible. At last it too vanished, and only the sea was to be seen, rippling in the moonlight.

The pilgrims lay down to sleep, and all was quiet on deck.

75

The Bishop did not wish to sleep, but sat alone at the stern, gazing at the sea where the island was no longer visible, and thinking of the good old men. He thought how pleased they had been to learn the Lord's Prayer; and he thanked God for having sent him to teach and help such godly men.

So the Bishop sat, thinking, and gazing at the sea where the island had disappeared. And the moonlight flickered before his eyes, sparkling, now here, now there, upon the waves. Suddenly he saw something white and shining, on the bright path which the moon cast across the sea. Was it a seagull, or the little gleaming sail of some small boat? The Bishop fixed his eyes on it, wondering.

"It must be a boat sailing after us," thought he, "but it is overtaking us very rapidly. It was far, far away a minute ago, but now it is much nearer. It cannot be a boat, for I can see no sail; but whatever it may be, it is following us and catching us up."

And he could not make out what it was. Not a boat, nor a bird, nor a fish! It was too large for a man, and besides a man could not be out there in the midst of the sea. The Bishop rose, and said to the helmsman:

"Look there, what is that, my friend? What is it?" the Bishop repeated, though he could now see plainly what it was—the three hermits running upon the water, all gleaming white, their grey beards shining, and approaching the ship as quickly as though it were not moving.

The steersman looked, and let go the helm in terror.

"Oh, Lord! The hermits are running after us on the water as though it were dry land!"

The passengers, hearing him, jumped up and crowded to the stern. They saw the hermits coming along hand in hand, and the two outer ones beckoning the ship to stop. All three were gliding along upon the water without moving their feet.

76

Before the ship could be stopped, the hermits had reached it, and raising their heads, all three as with one voice, began to say:

"We have forgotten your teaching, servant of God. As long as we kept repeating it we remembered, but when we stopped saying it for a time, a word dropped out, and now it has all gone to pieces. We can remember nothing of it. Teach us again."

The Bishop crossed himself, and leaning over the ship's side, said:

"Your own prayer will reach the Lord, men of God. It is not for me to teach you. Pray for us sinners."

And the Bishop bowed low before the old men; and they turned and went back across the sea. And a light shone until daybreak on the spot where they were lost to sight.

1886.

Where Love Is, God Is

IN a certain town there lived a cobbler, Martin Avdéich by
name. He had a tiny room in a basement, the one window
of which looked out on to the street. Through it one could only
see the feet of those who passed by, but Martin recognized the

people by their boots. He had lived long in the place and had many acquaintances. There was hardly a pair of boots in the neighborhood that had not been once or twice through his hands, so he often saw his own handiwork through the window. Some he had resoled, some patched, some stitched up, and to some he had even put fresh uppers. He had plenty to do, for he worked well, used good material, did not charge too much, and could be relied on. If he could do a job by the day required, he undertook it; if not, he told the truth and gave no false promises; so he was well known and never short of work.

Martin had always been a good man, but in his old age he began to think more about his soul and to draw nearer to God. While he still worked for a master, before he set up on his own account, his wife had died, leaving him with a three-year-old son. None of his elder children had lived, they had all died in infancy. At first Martin thought of sending his little son to his sister's in the country, but then he felt sorry to part with the boy, thinking: "It would be hard for my little Kapitón to have to grow up in a strange family, I will keep him with me."

Martin left his master and went into lodgings with his little son. But he had no luck with his children. No sooner had the boy reached an age when he could help his father and be a support as well as a joy to him, than he fell ill and, after being laid up for a week with a burning fever, died. Martin buried his son, and gave way to despair so great and overwhelming that he murmured against God. In his sorrow he prayed again and again that he too might die, reproaching God for having taken the son he loved, his only son, while he, old as he was, remained alive. After that Martin left off going to church.

One day an old man from Martin's native village, who had been a pilgrim for the last eight years, called in on his way from the Tróitsa Monastery. Martin opened his heart to him and told him of his sorrow.

"I no longer even wish to live, holy man," he said. "All I ask of God is that I soon may die. I am now quite without hope in the world."

The old man replied: "You have no right to say such things, Martin. We cannot judge God's ways. Not our reasoning, but God's will, decides. If God willed that your son should die and you should live, it must be best so. As to your despair—that comes because you wish to live for your own happiness."

"What else should one live for?" asked Martin.

"For God, Martin," said the old man. "He gives you life, and you must live for Him. When you have learnt to live for Him, you will grieve no more, and all will seem easy to you."

Martin was silent awhile, and then asked: "But how is one to live for God?"

The old man answered: "How one may live for God has been shown us by Christ. Can you read? Then buy the Gospels and read them: there you will see how God would have you live. You have it all there."

These words sank deep into Martin's heart, and that same day he went and bought himself a Testament in large print, and began to read.

At first he meant only to read on holidays, but having once begun he found it made his heart so light that he read every day. Sometimes he was so absorbed in his reading that the oil in his lamp burnt out before he could tear himself away from the book. He continued to read every night, and the more he read the more clearly he understood what God required of him, and how he might live for God. And his heart grew lighter and lighter. Before, when he went to bed he used to lie with a heavy heart, moaning as he thought of his little Kapitón; but now he only repeated again and again: "Glory to Thee, glory to Thee, O Lord! Thy will be done!"

From that time Martin's whole life changed. Formerly, on

83

holidays he used to go and have tea at the public-house and did not even refuse a glass or two of vódka. Sometimes, after having had a drop with a friend, he left the public-house not drunk, but rather merry, and would say foolish things: shout at a man, or abuse him. Now all that sort of thing passed away from him. His life became peaceful and joyful. He sat down to his work in the morning, and when he had finished his day's work he took the lamp down from the wall, stood it on the table, fetched his book from the shelf, opened it, and sat down to read. The more he read the better he understood and the clearer and happier he felt in his mind.

It happened once that Martin sat up late, absorbed in his book. He was reading Luke's Gospel; and in the sixth chapter he came upon the verses:

"To him that smiteth thee on the one cheek offer also the other; and from him that taketh away thy cloke withhold not thy coat also. Give to every man that asketh thee; and of him that taketh away thy goods ask them not again. And as ye would that men should do to you, do ye also to them likewise."

He also read the verses where our Lord says:

"And why call ye me, Lord, Lord, and do not the things which I say? Whosoever cometh to me, and heareth my sayings, and doeth them, I will shew you to whom he is like: He is like a man which built an house, and digged deep, and laid the foundation on a rock: and when the flood arose, the stream beat vehemently upon that house, and could not shake it: for it was founded upon a rock. But he that heareth, and doeth not, is like a man that without a foundation built an house upon the earth, against which the stream did beat vehemently, and immediately it fell; and the ruin of that house was great."

When Martin read these words his soul was glad within him. He took off his spectacles and laid them on the book, and leaning his elbows on the table pondered over what he had read.

84

He tried his own life by the standard of those words, asking himself:

"Is my house built on the rock, or on sand? If it stands on the rock, it is well. It seems easy enough while one sits here alone, and one thinks one has done all that God commands; but as soon as I cease to be on my guard, I sin again. Still I will persevere. It brings such joy. Help me, O Lord!"

He thought all this, and was about to go to bed, but was loth to leave his book. So he went on reading the seventh chapter—about the centurion, the widow's son, and the answer to John's disciples—and he came to the part where a rich Pharisee invited the Lord to his house; and he read how the woman who was a sinner anointed his feet and washed them with her tears, and how he justified her. Coming to the forty-fourth verse, he read:

"And turning to the woman, he said unto Simon, Seest thou this woman? I entered into thine house, thou gavest me no water for my feet: but she hath wetted my feet with her tears, and wiped them with her hair. Thou gavest me no kiss; but she, since the time I came in, hath not ceased to kiss my feet. My head with oil thou didst not anoint: but she hath anointed my feet with ointment."

He read these verses and thought: "He gave no water for his feet, gave no kiss, his head with oil he did not anoint. . . ." And Martin took off his spectacles once more, laid them on his book, and pondered.

"He must have been like me, that Pharisee. He too thought only of himself—how to get a cup of tea, how to keep warm and comfortable; never a thought of his guest. He took care of himself, but for his guest he cared nothing at all. Yet who was the guest? The Lord himself! If he came to me, should I behave like that?"

Then Martin laid his head upon both his arms and, before he was aware of it, he fell asleep.

"Martin!" he suddenly heard a voice, as if some one had breathed the word above his ear.

He started from his sleep. "Who's there?" he asked.

He turned round and looked at the door; no one was there. He called again. Then he heard quite distinctly: "Martin, Martin! Look out into the street to-morrow, for I shall come."

Martin roused himself, rose from his chair and rubbed his eyes, but did not know whether he had heard these words in a dream or awake. He put out the lamp and lay down to sleep.

Next morning he rose before daylight and after saying his prayers he lit the fire and prepared his cabbage soup and buckwheat porridge. Then he lit the samovár,[1] put on his apron, and sat down by the window to his work. As he sat working Martin thought over what had happened the night before. At times it seemed to him like a dream, and at times he thought that he had really heard the voice. "Such things have happened before now," thought he.

So he sat by the window, looking out into the street more than he worked, and whenever any one passed in unfamiliar boots he would stoop and look up, so as to see not the feet only but the face of the passer-by as well. A house-porter passed in new felt boots; then a water-carrier. Presently an old soldier of Nicholas' reign came near the window, spade in hand. Martin knew him by his boots, which were shabby old felt ones, goloshed with leather. The old man was called Stepánich: a neighboring tradesman kept him in his house for charity, and his duty was to help the house-porter. He began to clear away the snow before Martin's window. Martin glanced at him and then went on with his work.

1 The samovár ("self-boiler") is an urn in which water can be heated and kept on the boil.

"I must be growing crazy with age," said Martin, laughing at his fancy. "Stepánich comes to clear away the snow, and I must needs imagine it's Christ coming to visit me. Old dotard that I am!"

Yet after he had made a dozen stitches he felt drawn to look out of the window again. He saw that Stepánich had leaned his spade against the wall and was either resting himself or trying to get warm. The man was old and broken down, and had evidently not enough strength even to clear away the snow.

"What if I called him in and gave him some tea?" thought Martin. "The samovár is just on the boil."

He stuck his awl in its place, and rose; and putting the samovár on the table, made tea. Then he tapped the window with his fingers. Stepánich turned and came to the window. Martin beckoned to him to come in and went himself to open the door.

"Come in," he said, "and warm yourself a bit. I'm sure you must be cold."

"May God bless you!" Stepánich answered. "My bones do ache to be sure." He came in, first shaking off the snow, and lest he should leave marks on the floor he began wiping his feet, but as he did so he tottered and nearly fell.

"Don't trouble to wipe your feet," said Martin; "I'll wipe up the floor—it's all in the day's work. Come, friend, sit down and have some tea."

Filling two tumblers, he passed one to his visitor, and pouring his own out into the saucer, began to blow on it.

Stepánich emptied his glass, and, turning it upside down,[1] put the remains of his piece of sugar on the top. He began to express his thanks, but it was plain that he would be glad of some more.

[1] Turning the glass upside down was the customary way of intimating that one had had enough.

"Have another glass," said Martin, refilling the visitor's tumbler and his own. But while he drank his tea Martin kept looking out into the street.

"Are you expecting any one?" asked the visitor.

"Am I expecting any one? Well now, I'm ashamed to tell you. It isn't that I really expect any one; but I heard something last night which I can't get out of my mind. Whether it was a vision, or only a fancy, I can't tell. You see, friend, last night I was reading the Gospel, about Christ the Lord, how he suffered and how he walked on earth. You have heard tell of it, I dare say."

"I have heard tell of it," answered Stepánich; "but I'm an ignorant man and not able to read."

"Well, you see, I was reading of how he walked on earth. I came to that part, you know, where he went to a Pharisee who did not receive him well. Well, friend, as I read about it, I thought how that man did not receive Christ the Lord with proper honor. Suppose such a thing could happen to such a man as myself, I thought, what would I not do to receive him! But that man gave him no reception at all. Well, friend, as I was thinking of this I began to doze, and as I dozed I heard some one call me by name. I got up, and thought I heard some one whispering, 'Expect me; I will come to-morrow.' This happened twice over. And to tell you the truth, it sank so into my mind that, though I am ashamed of it myself, I keep on expecting him, the dear Lord!"

Stepánich shook his head in silence, finished his tumbler and laid it on its side; but Martin stood it up again and refilled it for him.

"Here, drink another glass, bless you! And I was thinking, too, how he walked on earth and despised no one, but went mostly among common folk. He went with plain people, and chose his disciples from among the likes of us, from workmen

88

like us, sinners that we are. 'He who raises himself,' he said, 'shall be humbled; and he who humbles himself shall be raised.' 'You call me Lord,' he said, 'and I will wash your feet.' 'He who would be first,' he said, 'let him be the servant of all; because,' he said, 'blessed are the poor, the humble, the meek, and the merciful.' "

Stepánich forgot his tea. He was an old man, easily moved to tears, and as he sat and listened the tears ran down his cheeks.

"Come, drink some more," said Martin. But Stepánich crossed himself, thanked him, moved away his tumbler, and rose.

"Thank you, Martin Avdéich," he said, "you have given me food and comfort both for soul and body."

"You're very welcome. Come again another time. I am glad to have a guest," said Martin.

Stepánich went away; and Martin poured out the last of the tea and drank it up. Then he put away the tea things and sat down to his work, stitching the back seam of a boot. And as he stitched he kept looking out of the window, waiting for Christ and thinking about him and his doings. And his head was full of Christ's sayings.

Two soldiers went by: one in Government boots, the other in boots of his own; then the master of a neighboring house, in shining goloshes; then a baker carrying a basket. All these passed on. Then a woman came up in worsted stockings and peasant-made shoes. She passed the window, but stopped by the wall. Martin glanced up at her through the window and saw that she was a stranger, poorly dressed and with a baby in her arms. She stopped by the wall with her back to the wind, trying to wrap the baby up though she had hardly anything to wrap it in. The woman had only summer clothes on, and even they were shabby and worn. Through the window Martin heard the baby crying, and the woman trying to soothe it but unable

89

to do so. Martin rose, and going out of the door and up the steps he called to her.

"My dear, I say, my dear!"

The woman heard and turned round.

"Why do you stand out there with the baby in the cold? Come inside. You can wrap him up better in a warm place. Come this way!"

The woman was surprised to see an old man in an apron, with spectacles on his nose, calling to her, but she followed him in.

They went down the steps, entered the little room, and the old man led her to the bed.

"There, sit down, my dear, near the stove. Warm yourself and feed the baby."

"Haven't any milk. I have eaten nothing myself since early morning," said the woman, but still she took the baby to her breast.

Martin shook his head. He brought out a basin and some bread. Then he opened the oven door and poured some cabbage soup into the basin. He took out the porridge pot also, but the porridge was not yet ready, so he spread a cloth on the table and served only the soup and bread.

"Sit down and eat, my dear, and I'll mind the baby. Why, bless me, I've had children of my own; I know how to manage them."

The woman crossed herself, and sitting down at the table began to eat, while Martin put the baby on the bed and sat down by it. He chucked and chucked, but having no teeth he could not do it well and the baby continued to cry. Then Martin tried poking at him with his finger; he drove his finger straight at the baby's mouth and then quickly drew it back, and did this again and again. He did not let the baby take his finger in its mouth, because it was all black with cobbler's wax. But the baby

90

first grew quiet watching the finger, and then began to laugh. And Martin felt quite pleased.

The woman sat eating and talking, and told him who she was, and where she had been.

"I'm a soldier's wife," said she. "They sent my husband somewhere, far away, eight months ago, and I have heard nothing of him since. I had a place as cook till my baby was born, but then they would not keep me with a child. For three months now I have been struggling, unable to find a place, and I've had to sell all I had for food. I tried to go as a wet-nurse, but no one would have me; they said I was too starved-looking and thin. Now I have just been to see a tradesman's wife (a woman from our village is in service with her) and she has promised to take me. I thought it was all settled at last, but she tells me not to come till next week. It is far to her place, and I am fagged out, and baby is quite starved, poor mite. Fortunately our landlady has pity on us, and lets us lodge free, else I don't know what we should do."

Martin sighed. "Haven't you any warmer clothing?" he asked.

"How could I get warm clothing?" said she. "Why, I pawned my last shawl for sixpence yesterday."

Then the woman came and took the child, and Martin got up. He went and looked among some things that were hanging on the wall, and brought back an old cloak.

"Here," he said, "though it's a worn-out old thing, it will do to wrap him up in."

The woman looked at the cloak, then at the old man, and taking it, burst into tears. Martin turned away, and groping under the bed brought out a small trunk. He fumbled about in it, and again sat down opposite the woman. And the woman said:

"The Lord bless you, friend. Surely Christ must have sent

91

me to your window, else the child would have frozen. It was mild when I started, but now see how cold it has turned. Surely it must have been Christ who made you look out of your window and take pity on me, poor wretch!"

Martin smiled and said, "It is quite true; it was He made me do it. It was no mere chance made me look out."

And he told the woman his dream, and how he had heard the Lord's voice promising to visit him that day.

"Who knows? All things are possible," said the woman. And she got up and threw the cloak over her shoulders, wrapping it round herself and round the baby. Then she bowed, and thanked Martin once more.

"Take this for Christ's sake," said Martin, and gave her six-pence to get her shawl out of pawn. The woman crossed herself, and Martin did the same, and then he saw her out.

After the woman had gone, Martin ate some cabbage soup, cleared the things away, and sat down to work again. He sat and worked, but did not forget the window, and every time a shadow fell on it he looked up at once to see who was passing. People he knew and strangers passed by, but no one remarkable.

After a while Martin saw an apple-woman stop just in front of his window. She had a large basket, but there did not seem to be many apples left in it; she had evidently sold most of her stock. On her back she had a sack full of chips, which she was taking home. No doubt she had gathered them at some place where building was going on. The sack evidently hurt her and she wanted to shift it from one shoulder to the other, so she put it down on the footpath and, placing her basket on a post, began to shake down the chips in the sack. While she was doing this a boy in a tattered cap ran up, snatched an apple out of the basket and tried to slip away; but the old woman noticed it and, turning, caught the boy by his sleeve. He began to struggle, trying to free himself, but the old woman held on with both

92

hands, knocked his cap off his head, and seized hold of his hair. The boy screamed and the old woman scolded. Martin dropped his awl, not waiting to stick it in its place, and rushed out of the door. Stumbling up the steps, and dropping his spectacles in his hurry, he ran out into the street. The old woman was pulling the boy's hair and scolding him, and threatening to take him to the police. The lad was struggling and protesting, saying, "I did not take it. What are you beating me for? Let me go!"

Martin separated them. He took the boy by the hand and said, "Let him go, Granny. Forgive him for Christ's sake."

"I'll pay him out, so that he won't forget it for a year! I'll take the rascal to the police!"

Martin began entreating the old woman.

"Let him go, Granny. He won't do it again. Let him go for Christ's sake!"

The old woman let go, and the boy wished to run away, but Martin stopped him.

"Ask the Granny's forgiveness!" said he. "And don't do it another time. I saw you take the apple."

The boy began to cry and to beg pardon.

"That's right. And now here's an apple for you," and Martin took an apple from the basket and gave it to the boy, saying, "I will pay you, Granny."

"You will spoil them that way, the young rascals," said the old woman. "He ought to be whipped so that he should remember it for a week."

"Oh, Granny, Granny," said Martin, "that's our way—but it's not God's way. If he should be whipped for stealing an apple, what should be done to us for our sins?"

The old woman was silent.

And Martin told her the parable of the lord who forgave his servant a large debt, and how the servant went out and seized

93

his debtor by the throat. The old woman listened to it all, and the boy, too, stood by and listened.

"God bids us forgive," said Martin, "or else we shall not be forgiven. Forgive every one, and a thoughtless youngster most of all."

The old woman wagged her head and sighed.

"It's true enough," said she, "but they are getting terribly spoilt."

"Then we old ones must show them better ways," Martin replied.

"That's just what I say," said the old woman. "I have had seven of them myself, and only one daughter is left." And the old woman began to tell how and where she was living with her daughter, and how many grandchildren she had. "There now," she said, "I have but little strength left, yet I work hard for the sake of my grandchildren; and nice children they are, too. No one comes out to meet me but the children. Little Annie, now, won't leave me for any one. 'It's grandmother, dear grandmother, darling grandmother.'" And the old woman completely softened at the thought.

"Of course it was only his childishness, God help him," said she, referring to the boy.

As the old woman was about to hoist her sack on her back, the lad sprang forward to her, saying, "Let me carry it for you, Granny. I'm going that way."

The old woman nodded her head, and put the sack on the boy's back, and they went down the street together, the old woman quite forgetting to ask Martin to pay for the apple. Martin stood and watched them as they went along talking to each other.

When they were out of sight Martin went back to the house. Having found his spectacles unbroken on the steps, he picked up his awl and sat down again to work. He worked a little, but could soon not see to pass the bristle through the holes in the leather; and presently he noticed the lamplighter passing on his way to light the street lamps.

"Seems it's time to light up," thought he. So he trimmed his lamp, hung it up, and sat down again to work. He finished off one boot and, turning it about, examined it. It was all right. Then he gathered his tools together, swept up the cuttings, put away the bristles and the thread and the awls, and, taking down the lamp, placed it on the table. Then he took the Gospels from the shelf. He meant to open them at the place he had marked the day before with a bit of morocco, but the book opened at another place. As Martin opened it, his yesterday's dream came back to his mind, and no sooner had he thought of it than he seemed to hear footsteps, as though some one were moving behind him. Martin turned round, and it seemed to him as if people were standing in the dark corner, but he could not make out who they were. And a voice whispered in his ear: "Martin, Martin, don't you know me?"

"Who is it?" muttered Martin.

"It is I," said the voice. And out of the dark corner stepped Stepánich, who smiled, and vanishing like a cloud was seen no more.

"It is I," said the voice again. And out of the darkness stepped the woman with the baby in her arms, and the woman smiled and the baby laughed, and they too vanished.

"It is I," said the voice once more. And the old woman and the boy with the apple stepped out and both smiled, and then they too vanished.

And Martin's soul grew glad. He crossed himself, put on his spectacles, and began reading the Gospel just where it had opened; and at the top of the page he read:

"I was an hungered, and ye gave me meat: I was thirsty, and ye gave me drink: I was a stranger, and ye took me in."

95

And at the bottom of the page he read:

"Inasmuch as ye did it unto one of these my brethren, even these least, ye did it unto me" (*Matt.* xxv).

And Martin understood that his dream had come true; and that the Saviour had really come to him that day, and he had welcomed him.

1885.

Two Old Men

"*The woman saith unto him, Sir, I perceive that thou art a prophet. Our fathers worshipped in this mountain, and ye say, that in Jerusalem is the place where men ought to worship. Jesus saith unto her, Woman, believe me, the hour cometh when neither in this mountain, nor in Jerusalem, shall ye worship the Father. . . . But the hour cometh, and now is, when the true worshippers shall worship the Father in spirit and truth: for such doth the Father seek to be his worshippers.*"
—John iv. 19-21, 23.

THERE were once two old men who decided to go on a pilgrimage to worship God at Jerusalem. One of them was a well-to-do peasant named Efím Tarásich Shevélev. The other, Elisha Bódrov, was not so well off.

99

Efím was a staid man, serious and firm. He neither drank nor smoked nor took snuff, and had never used bad language in his life. He had twice served as village Elder, and when he left office his accounts were in good order. He had a large family: two sons and a married grandson, all living with him. He was hale, long-bearded, and erect, and it was only when he was past sixty that a little grey began to show itself in his beard.

Elisha was neither rich nor poor. He had formerly gone out carpentering, but now that he was growing old he stayed at home and kept bees. One of his sons had gone away to find work, the other was living at home. Elisha was a kindly and cheerful old man. It is true he drank sometimes, and he took snuff, and was fond of singing; but he was a peaceable man and lived on good terms with his family and with his neighbors. He was short and dark, with a curly beard, and, like his patron saint Elisha, he was quite bald-headed.

The two old men had taken a vow long since and had arranged to go on a pilgrimage to Jerusalem together: but Efím could never spare the time; he always had so much business on hand: as soon as one thing was finished he started another. First he had to arrange his grandson's marriage; then to wait for his youngest son's return from the army, and after that he began building a new hut.

One holiday the two old men met outside the hut and, sitting down on some timber, began to talk.

"Well," asked Elisha, "when are we to fulfill our vow?"

Efím made a wry face.

"We must wait," he said. "This year has turned out a hard one for me. I started building this hut thinking it would cost me something over a hundred rúbles, but now it's getting on for three hundred and it's still not finished. We shall have to wait till the summer. In summer, God willing, we will go without fail."

100

"It seems to me we ought not to put it off, but should go at once," said Elisha. "Spring is the best time."

"The time's right enough, but what about my building? How can I leave that?"

"As if you had no one to leave in charge! Your son can look after it."

"But how? My eldest son is not trustworthy—he sometimes takes a glass too much."

"Ah, neighbor, when we die they'll get on without us. Let your son begin now to get some experience."

"That's true enough; but somehow when one begins a thing one likes to see it done."

"Eh, friend, we can never get through all we have to do. The other day the women-folk at home were washing and house-cleaning for Easter. Here something needed doing, there something else, and they could not get everything done. So my eldest daughter-in-law, who's a sensible woman, says: 'We may be thankful the holiday comes without waiting for us, or however hard we worked we should never be ready for it.' "

Efím became thoughtful.

"I've spent a lot of money on this building," he said, "and one can't start on the journey with empty pockets. We shall want a hundred rúbles apiece—and it's no small sum."

Elisha laughed.

"Now, come, come, old friend!" he said, "you have ten times as much as I, and yet you talk about money. Only say when we are to start, and though I have nothing now I shall have enough by then."

Efím also smiled.

"Dear me, I did not know you were so rich!" said he. "Why, where will you get it from?"

"I can scrape some together at home, and if that's not enough,

I'll sell half a score of hives to my neighbor. He's long been wanting to buy them."

"If they swarm well this year, you'll regret it."

"Regret it! Not I, neighbor! I never regretted anything in my life, except my sins. There's nothing more precious than the soul."

"That's so; still it's not right to neglect things at home."

"But what if our souls are neglected? That's worse. We took the vow, so let us go! Now, seriously, let us go!"

I I

Elisha succeeded in persuading his comrade. In the morning after thinking it well over, Efím came to Elisha.

"You are right," said he, "let us go. Life and death are in God's hands. We must go now, while we are still alive and have the strength."

A week later the old men were ready to start. Efím had money enough at hand. He took a hundred rúbles himself, and left two hundred with his wife.

Elisha, too, got ready. He sold ten hives to his neighbor, with any new swarms that might come from them before the summer. He took seventy rúbles for the lot. The rest of the hundred rúbles he scraped together from the other members of his household, fairly clearing them all out. His wife gave him all she had been saving up for her funeral, and his daughter-in-law also gave him what she had.

Efím gave his eldest son definite orders about everything: when and how much grass to mow, where to cart the manure, and how to finish off and roof the cottage. He thought out everything, and gave his orders accordingly. Elisha, on the other hand, only explained to his wife that she was to keep separate the swarms from the hives he had sold and to be sure to let the

102

neighbor have them all, without any tricks. As to household affairs, he did not even mention them.

"You will see what to do and how to do it as the needs arise," he said. "You are the masters and will know how to do what's best for yourselves."

So the old men got ready. Their people baked them cakes, and made bags for them, and cut them linen for leg-bands.[1] They put on new leather shoes and took with them spare shoes of platted bark. Their families went with them to the end of the village and there took leave of them, and the old men started on their pilgrimage.

Elisha left home in a cheerful mood and as soon as he was out of the village forgot all his home affairs. His only care was how to please his comrade, how to avoid saying a rude word to any one, how to get to his destination and home again in peace and love. Walking along the road, Elisha would either whisper some prayer to himself or go over in his mind such of the lives of the saints as he was able to remember. When he came across any one on the road, or turned in anywhere for the night, he tried to behave as gently as possible and to say a godly word. So he journeyed on, rejoicing. One thing only he could not do: he could not give up taking snuff. Though he had left his snuff-box behind, he hankered after it. Then a man he met on the road gave him some snuff, and every now and then he would lag behind (not to lead his comrade into temptation) and would take a pinch of snuff.

Efím too walked well and firmly, doing no wrong and speaking no vain words, but his heart was not so light. Household cares weighed on his mind. He kept worrying about what was going on at home. Had he not forgotten to give his son this or that order? Would his son do things properly? If he happened to see potatoes being planted or manure carted as he went along,

[1] Worn by Russian peasants instead of stockings.

103

he wondered if his son was doing as he had been told. And he almost wanted to turn back and show him how to do things, or even do them himself.

III

The old men had been walking for five weeks, they had worn out their home-made bark shoes and had to begin buying new ones when they reached Little Russia.[1] From the time they left home they had had to pay for their food and for their night's lodging, but when they reached Little Russia the people vied with one another in asking them into their huts. They took them in and fed them, and would accept no payment; and more than that, they put bread or even cakes into their bags for them to eat on the road.

The old men traveled some five hundred miles in this manner free of expense, but after they had crossed the next province, they came to a district where the harvest had failed. The peasants still gave them free lodging at night, but no longer fed them for nothing. Sometimes even they could get no bread: they offered to pay for it, but there was none to be had. The people said the harvest had completely failed the year before. Those who had been rich were ruined and had had to sell all they possessed; those of moderate means were left destitute, and those of the poor who had not left those parts, wandered about begging, or starved at home in utter want. In the winter they had had to eat husks and goosefoot.

One night the old men stopped in a small village; they bought fifteen pounds of bread, slept there, and started before sunrise to get well on their way before the heat of the day. When

[1] Little Russia is situated in the south-western part of Russia, and consists of the Governments of Kíev, Poltáva, Chernígov, and part of Kharkov and Kherson; it is now generally called the Ukraine.

104

they had gone some eight miles, on coming to a stream they sat down, and, filling a bowl with water, they steeped some bread in it and ate it. Then they changed their leg-bands and rested for a while. Elisha took out his snuff. Efím shook his head at him.

"How is it you don't give up that nasty habit?" said he.

Elisha waved his hand. "The evil habit is stronger than I," he said.

Presently they got up and went on. After walking for nearly another eight miles, they came to a large village and passed right through it. It had now grown hot. Elisha was tired out and wanted to rest and have a drink, but Efím did not stop. Efím was the better walker of the two and Elisha found it hard to keep up with him.

"If I could only have a drink," said he.

"Well, have a drink," said Efím. "I don't want any."

Elisha stopped.

"You go on," he said, "but I'll just run in to the little hut there. I will catch you up in a moment."

"All right," said Efím, and he went on along the high road alone while Elisha turned back to the hut.

It was a small hut plastered with clay, the bottom a dark color, the top whitewashed; but the clay had crumbled away. Evidently it was long since it had been replastered, and the thatch was off the roof on one side. The entrance to the hut was through the yard. Elisha entered the yard, and saw, lying close to a bank of earth that ran round the hut, a gaunt, beardless man with his shirt tucked into his trousers, as is the custom in Little Russia.[1] The man must have lain down in the shade, but the sun had come round and now shone full on him. Though not asleep, he still lay there. Elisha called to him and asked for a drink, but the man gave no answer.

[1] In Great Russia the peasants let their shirt hang outside their trousers.

"He is either ill or unfriendly," thought Elisha; and going to the door he heard a child crying in the hut. He took hold of the ring that served as a door-handle and knocked with it.

"Hey, masters!" he called. No answer. He knocked again with his staff.

"Hey, Christians!" Nothing stirred.

"Hey, servants of God!" Still no reply.

Elisha was about to turn away, when he thought he heard a groan the other side of the door.

"Dear me, some misfortune must have happened to the people! I had better have a look."

And Elisha entered the hut.

IV

Elisha turned the ring, the door was not fastened. He opened it and went along up the narrow passage. The door into the dwelling-room was open. To the left was a brick stove; in front against the wall was an icon-shelf [1] and a table before it; by the table was a bench on which sat an old woman, bareheaded and wearing only a single garment. There she sat with her head resting on the table, and near her was a thin, wax-colored boy, with a protruding stomach. He was asking for something, pulling at her sleeve and crying bitterly. Elisha entered. The air in the hut was very foul. He looked round, and saw a woman lying on the floor behind the stove: she lay flat on the ground with her eyes closed and her throat rattling, now stretching out a leg, now dragging it in, tossing from side to side; and the foul smell came from her. Evidently she could do nothing for herself and no one had been attending to her needs. The old woman lifted her head and saw the stranger.

[1] An icon (properly ikón) is a representation of God, Christ, an angel, or a saint, or of a sacred event, usually painted, enameled, or embossed.

106

"What do you want?" said she. "What do you want, man? We have nothing."

Elisha understood her, though she spoke in the Little Russian dialect.

"I came in for a drink of water, servant of God," he said.

"There's no one—no one—we have nothing to fetch it in. Go your way."

Then Elisha asked:

"Is there no one among you, then, well enough to attend to that woman?"

"No, we have no one. My son is dying outside, and we are dying in here."

The little boy had ceased crying when he saw the stranger, but when the old woman began to speak, he began again, and clutching hold of her sleeve cried:

"Bread, Granny, bread."

Elisha was about to question the old woman, when the man staggered into the hut. He came along the passage clinging to the wall, but as he was entering the dwelling-room he fell in the corner near the threshold, and without trying to get up again to reach the bench, he began to speak in broken words. He brought out a word at a time, stopping to draw breath, and gasping.

"Illness has seized us . . ." said he, "and famine. He is dying . . . of hunger."

And he motioned towards the boy and began to sob.

Elisha jerked up the sack behind his shoulder and, pulling the straps off his arms, put it on the floor. Then he lifted it on to the bench and untied the strings. Having opened the sack, he took out a loaf of bread and, cutting off a piece with his knife, handed it to the man. The man would not take it, but pointed to the little boy and to a little girl crouching behind the stove, as if to say:

107

"Give it to them."

Elisha held it out to the boy. When the boy smelt bread, he stretched out his arms, and seizing the slice with both his little hands, bit into it so that his nose disappeared in the chunk. The little girl came out from behind the stove and fixed her eyes on the bread. Elisha gave her also a slice. Then he cut off another piece and gave it to the old woman, and she too began munching it.

"If only some water could be brought," she said, "their mouths are parched. I tried to fetch some water yesterday—or was it to-day—I can't remember, but I fell down and could go no further, and the pail has remained there, unless some one has taken it."

Elisha asked where the well was. The old woman told him. Elisha went out, found the pail, brought some water, and gave the people a drink. The children and the old woman ate some more bread with the water, but the man would not eat.

"I cannot eat," he said.

All this time the younger woman did not show any consciousness, but continued to toss from side to side. Presently Elisha went to the village shop and bought some millet, salt, flour, and oil. He found an axe, chopped some wood, and made a fire. The little girl came and helped him. Then he boiled some soup and gave the starving people a meal.

V

The man ate a little, the old woman had some too, and the little girl and boy licked the bowl clean and then curled up and fell fast asleep in one another's arms.

The man and the old woman then began telling Elisha how they had sunk to their present state.

"We were poor enough before," said they, "but when the

108

crops failed, what we gathered hardly lasted us through the autumn. We had nothing left by the time winter came, and had to beg from the neighbors and from any one we could. At first they gave, then they began to refuse. Some would have been glad enough to help us but had nothing to give. And we were ashamed of asking: we were in debt all round, and owed money, and flour, and bread."

"I went to look for work," the man said, "but could find none. Everywhere people were offering to work merely for their own keep. One day you'd get a short job and then you might spend two days looking for work. Then the old woman and the girl went begging, further away. But they got very little; bread was so scarce. Still we scraped food together somehow and hoped to struggle through till next harvest, but towards spring people ceased to give anything. And then this illness seized us. Things became worse and worse. One day we might have something to eat, and then nothing for two days. We began eating grass. Whether it was the grass, or what, made my wife ill, I don't know. She could not keep on her legs, and I had no strength left, and there was nothing to help us to recovery."

"I struggled on alone for a while," said the old woman, "but at last I broke down too for want of food, and grew quite weak. The girl also grew weak and timid. I told her to go to the neighbors—she would not leave the hut, but crept into a corner and sat there. The day before yesterday a neighbor looked in, but seeing that we were ill and hungry she turned away and left us. Her husband has had to go away and she has nothing for her own little ones to eat. And so we lay, waiting for death."

Having heard their story, Elisha gave up the thought of overtaking his comrade that day and remained with them all night. In the morning he got up and began doing the housework, just as if it were his own home. He kneaded the bread with the old

109

woman's help and lit the fire. Then he went with the little girl to the neighbors to get the most necessary things; for there was nothing in the hut, everything had been sold for bread—cooking utensils, clothing, and all. So Elisha began replacing what was necessary, making some things himself and buying some. He remained there one day, then another, and then a third. The little boy picked up strength and whenever Elisha sat down crept along the bench and nestled up to him. The little girl brightened up and helped in all the work, running after Elisha and calling,

"Daddy, daddy."

The old woman grew stronger and managed to go out to see a neighbor. The man too improved and was able to get about, holding on to the wall. Only the wife could not get up, but even she regained consciousness on the third day and asked for food.

"Well," thought Elisha, "I never expected to waste so much time on the way. Now I must be getting on."

V I

The fourth day was the feast day after the summer fast, and Elisha thought:

"I will stay and break the fast with these people. I'll go and buy them something and keep the feast with them, and to-morrow evening I will start."

So Elisha went into the village, bought milk, wheat-flour and dripping, and helped the old woman to boil and bake for the morrow. On the feast day Elisha went to church, and then broke the fast with his friends at the hut. That day the wife got up and managed to move about a bit. The husband had shaved and put on a clean shirt which the old woman had washed for him; and he went to beg for mercy of a rich peasant in the village to whom his ploughland and meadow were mortgaged.

110

He went to beg the rich peasant to grant him the use of the meadow and field till after the harvest; but in the evening he came back very sad and began to weep. The rich peasant had shown no mercy, but had said: "Bring me the money."

Elisha again grew thoughtful. "How are they to live now?" thought he to himself. "Other people will go haymaking, but there will be nothing for these to mow, their grass land is mortgaged. The rye will ripen. Others will reap (and what a fine crop mother earth is giving this year), but they have nothing to look forward to. Their three acres are pledged to the rich peasant. When I am gone they'll drift back into the state I found them in."

Elisha was in two minds, but finally decided not to leave that evening, but to wait until the morrow. He went out into the yard to sleep. He said his prayers and lay down; but he could not sleep. On the one hand he felt he ought to be going, for he had spent too much time and money as it was; on the other hand he felt sorry for the people.

"There seems to be no end to it," he said. "First I only meant to bring them a little water and give them each a slice of bread, and just see where it has landed me. It's a case of redeeming the meadow and the cornfield. And when I have done that I shall have to buy a cow for them, and a horse for the man to cart his sheaves. A nice coil you've got yourself into, brother Elisha! You've slipped your cables and lost your reckoning!"

Elisha got up, lifted his coat which he had been using for a pillow, unfolded it, got out his snuff and took a pinch, thinking that it might perhaps clear his thoughts.

But no! He thought and thought, and came to no conclusion. He ought to be going; and yet pity held him back. He did not know what to do. He refolded his coat and put it under his head again. He lay thus for a long time, till the cocks had already crowed once: then he was quite drowsy. And suddenly

111

it seemed as if some one had roused him. He saw that he was dressed for the journey, with the sack on his back and the staff in his hand, and the gate stood ajar so that he could just squeeze through. He was about to pass out when his sack caught against the fence on one side: he tried to free it, but then his leg-band caught on the other side and came undone. He pulled at the sack and saw that it had not caught on the fence, but that the little girl was holding it and crying,

"Bread, daddy, bread!"

He looked at his foot, and there was the tiny boy holding him by the leg-band, while the master of the hut and the old woman were looking at him through the window.

Elisha awoke and said to himself in an audible voice:

"To-morrow I will redeem their cornfield, and will buy them a horse, and flour to last till the harvest, and a cow for the little ones; or else while I go to seek the Lord beyond the sea I may lose Him in myself."

Then Elisha fell asleep and slept till morning. He awoke early, and going to the rich peasant, redeemed both the cornfield and the meadow land. He bought a scythe (for that also had been sold) and brought it back with him. Then he sent the man to mow, and himself went into the village. He heard that there was a horse and cart for sale at the public-house, and he struck a bargain with the owner and bought them. Then he bought a sack of flour, put it in the cart, and went to see about a cow. As he was going along he overtook two women talking as they went. Though they spoke the Little Russian dialect, he understood what they were saying.

"At first, it seems, they did not know him; they thought he was just an ordinary man. He came in to ask for a drink of water, and then he remained. Just think of the things he has bought for them! Why, they say he bought a horse and cart for them at the publican's only this morning! There are not many such men in the world. It's worth while going to have a look at him."

Elisha heard and understood that he was being praised, and he did not go to buy the cow, but returned to the inn, paid for the horse, harnessed it, drove up to the hut, and got out. The people in the hut were astonished when they saw the horse. They thought it might be for them, but dared not ask. The man came out to open the gate.

"Where did you get a horse from, grandfather?" he asked.

"Why, I bought it," said Elisha. "It was going cheap. Go and cut some grass and put it in the manger for it to eat during the night. And take in the sack."

The man unharnessed the horse, and carried the sack into the barn. Then he mowed some grass and put it in the manger. Everybody lay down to sleep. Elisha went outside and lay by the roadside. That evening he took his bag out with him. When every one was asleep, he got up, packed and fastened his bag, wrapped the linen bands round his legs, put on his shoes and coat, and set off to follow Efím.

VII

When Elisha had walked rather more than three miles it began to grow light. He sat down under a tree, opened his bag, counted his money, and found he had only seventeen rúbles and twenty kopéks left.

"Well," thought he, "it is no use trying to cross the sea with this. If I beg my way it may be worse than not going at all. Friend Efím will get to Jerusalem without me, and will place a candle at the shrines in my name. As for me, I'm afraid I shall never fulfill my vow in this life. I must be thankful it was made to a merciful Master and to one who pardons sinners."

Elisha rose, jerked his bag well up on his shoulders, and

113

turned back. Not wishing to be recognized by any one, he made a circuit to avoid the village, and walked briskly homeward. Coming from home the way had seemed difficult to him and he had found it hard to keep up with Efím, but now on his return journey, God helped him to get over the ground so that he hardly felt fatigue. Walking seemed like child's play. He went along swinging his staff and did his forty to fifty miles a day.

When Elisha reached home the harvest was over. His family were delighted to see him again, and all wanted to know what had happened: Why and how he had been left behind? And why he had returned without reaching Jerusalem? But Elisha did not tell them.

"It was not God's will that I should get there," said he. "I lost my money on the way and lagged behind my companion. Forgive me, for the Lord's sake!"

Elisha gave his old wife what money he had left. Then he questioned them about home affairs. Everything was going on well; all the work had been done, nothing neglected, and all were living in peace and concord.

Efím's family heard of his return the same day, and came for news of their old man, and to them Elisha gave the same answers.

"Efím is a fast walker. We parted three days before St. Peter's Day, and I meant to catch him up again, but all sorts of things happened. I lost my money and had no means to get any further, so I turned back."

The folks were astonished that so sensible a man should have acted so foolishly: should have started and not got to his destination, and should have squandered all his money. They wondered at it for a while and then forgot all about it; and Elisha forgot it too. He set to work again on his homestead. With his son's help he cut wood for fuel for the winter. He and the women threshed the corn. Then he mended the thatch on the

114

outhouses, put the bees under cover, and handed over to his neighbor the ten hives he had sold him in spring and all the swarms that had come from them. His wife tried not to tell how many swarms there had been from these hives, but Elisha knew well enough from which there had been swarms and from which not. And instead of ten, he handed over seventeen swarms to his neighbor. Having got everything ready for the winter, Elisha sent his son away to find work, while he himself took to plaiting shoes of bark and hollowing out logs for hives.

VIII

All that day while Elisha stopped behind in the hut with the sick people, Efím waited for him. He only went on a little way before he sat down. He waited and waited, had a nap, woke up again, and again sat waiting, but his comrade did not come. He gazed till his eyes ached. The sun was already sinking behind a tree and still no Elisha was to be seen.

"Perhaps he has passed me," thought Efím, "or perhaps some one gave him a lift and he drove by while I slept, and did not see me. But how could he help seeing me? One can see so far here in the steppe. Shall I go back? Suppose he is on in front we shall then miss each other completely and it will be still worse. I had better go on, and we shall be sure to meet where we put up for the night."

He came to a village, and told the watchman, if an old man of a certain description came along, to bring him to the hut where Efím stopped. But Elisha did not turn up that night. Efím went on, asking all he met whether they had not seen a little, bald-headed old man. No one had seen such a traveller. Efím wondered, but went on alone, saying:

"We shall be sure to meet in Odessa, or on board the ship," and he did not trouble more about it.

115

On the way he came across a pilgrim wearing a cassock, with long hair and a skull-cap such as priests wear. This pilgrim had been to Mount Athos, and was now going to Jerusalem for the second time. They both stopped at the same place one night and, having met, they travelled on together.

They got safely to Odessa and there had to wait three days for a ship. Many pilgrims from many different parts were in the same case. Again Efím asked about Elisha, but no one had seen him.

Efím got himself a foreign passport, which cost him five rúbles. He paid forty rúbles for a return ticket to Jerusalem, and bought a supply of bread and herrings for the voyage.

The pilgrim began explaining to Efím how he might get on to the ship without paying his fare, but Efím would not listen. "No, I came prepared to pay, and I shall pay," said he.

The ship was freighted and the pilgrims went on board, Efím and his new comrade among them. The anchors were weighed and the ship put out to sea.

All day they sailed smoothly, but towards night a wind arose, rain came on, and the vessel tossed about and shipped water. The people were frightened: the women wailed and screamed and some of the weaker men ran about the ship looking for shelter. Efím too was frightened, but he would not show it, and remained at the place on deck where he had settled down when first he came on board, beside some old men from Tambóv. There they sat silent, all night and all next day, holding on to their sacks. On the third day it grew calm, and on the fifth day they anchored at Constantinople. Some of the pilgrims went on shore to visit the Church of St. Sophia, now held by the Turks. Efím remained on the ship, and only bought some white bread. They lay there for twenty-four hours and then put to sea again. At Smyrna they stopped again, and at Alexandretta; but at last they arrived safely at Jaffa, where all the pilgrims had

116

to disembark. From there still it was more than forty miles by road to Jerusalem. When disembarking the people were again much frightened. The ship was high, and the people were dropped into boats, which rocked so much that it was easy to miss them and fall into the water. A couple of men did get a wetting, but at last all were safely landed.

They went on on foot, and at noon on the third day reached Jerusalem. They stopped outside the city, at the Russian hostel, where their passports were endorsed. Then, after dinner, Efím visited the Holy Places with his companion, the pilgrim. It was not the time when they could be admitted to the Holy Sepulchre, but they went to the Patriarchate. All the pilgrims assembled there. The women were separated from the men, who were all told to sit in a circle, barefoot. Then a monk came in with a towel to wash their feet. He washed, wiped, and then kissed their feet, and did this to every one in the circle. Efím's feet were washed and kissed, with the rest. He stood through vespers and matins, prayed, placed candles at the shrines, handed in booklets inscribed with his parents' names, that they might be mentioned in the church prayers. Here at the Patriarchate food and wine were given them. Next morning they went to the cell of Mary of Egypt, where she had lived doing penance. Here too they placed candles and had prayers read. From there they went to the Monastery of Abraham, and saw the place where Abraham intended to slay his son as an offering to God. Then they visited the spot where Christ appeared to Mary Magdalene, and the Church of James, the Lord's brother. The pilgrim showed Efím all these places, and told him how much money to give at each place. At mid-day they returned to the hostel and had dinner. As they were preparing to lie down and rest, the pilgrim cried out, and began to search his clothes, feeling them all over.

117

"My purse has been stolen, there were twenty-three rúbles in it," said he, "two ten-ruble notes and the rest in change."

He sighed and lamented a great deal, but as there was no help for it, they lay down to sleep.

IX

As Efím lay there he was assailed by temptation.

"No one has stolen any money from this pilgrim," thought he, "I do not believe he had any. He gave none away anywhere, though he made me give and even borrowed a rúble of me."

This thought had no sooner crossed his mind than Efím rebuked himself, saying: "What right have I to judge a man? It is a sin. I will think no more about it." But as soon as his thoughts began to wander, they turned again to the pilgrim: how interested he seemed to be in money, and how unlikely it sounded when he declared that his purse had been stolen.

"He never had any money," thought Efím. "It's all an invention."

Towards evening they got up, and went to midnight Mass at the great Church of the Resurrection, where the Lord's Sepulchre is. The pilgrim kept close to Efím and went everywhere with him. They came to the Church; a great many pilgrims were there, some Russians and some of other nationalities: Greeks, Armenians, Turks, and Syrians. Efím entered the Holy Gates with the crowd. A monk led them past the Turkish sentinels, to the place where the Saviour was taken down from the cross and anointed, and where candles were burning in nine great candlesticks. The monk showed and explained everything. Efím offered a candle there. Then the monk led Efím to the right, up the steps to Golgotha, to the place where the cross had stood. Efím prayed there. Then they showed him the cleft where the ground had been rent asunder to its nethermost

118

depths; then the place where Christ's hands and feet were nailed to the cross; then Adam's tomb, where the blood of Christ had dripped on to Adam's bones. Then they showed him the stone on which Christ sat when the crown of thorns was placed on His head; then the post to which Christ was bound when He was scourged. Then Efím saw the stone with two holes for Christ's feet. They were going to show him something else, but there was a stir in the crowd and the people all hurried to the Church of the Lord's Sepulchre itself. The Latin Mass had just finished there and the Russian liturgy was beginning. And Efím went with the crowd to the tomb cut in the rock.

He tried to get rid of the pilgrim, against whom he was still sinning in his mind, but the pilgrim would not leave him, but went with him to the Mass at the Holy Sepulchre. They tried to get to the front, but were too late. There was such a crowd that it was impossible to move either backwards or forwards. Efím stood looking in front of him, praying, and every now and then feeling for his purse. He was in two minds: sometimes he thought that the pilgrim was deceiving him, and then again he thought that if the pilgrim spoke the truth and his purse had really been stolen, the same thing might happen to himself.

X

Efím stood there gazing into the little chapel in which was the Holy Sepulchre itself with thirty-six lamps burning above it. As he stood looking over the people's heads, he saw something that surprised him. Just beneath the lamps in which the sacred fire burns, and in front of every one, Efím saw an old man in a grey coat, whose bald, shining head was just like Elisha Bódrov.

"It's like him," thought Efím, "but it cannot be Elisha. He could not have got ahead of me. The ship before ours started a

119

week earlier. He could not have caught that; and he was not on ours, for I saw every pilgrim on board."

Hardly had Efím thought this, when the little old man began to pray, and bowed three times: once forward to God, then once on each side—to the brethren. And as he turned his head to the right, Efím recognized him. It was Elisha Bódrov himself, with his dark, curly beard turning grey at the cheeks, with his brows, his eyes and nose, and his expression of face. Yes, it was he!

Efím was very pleased to have found his comrade again and wondered how Elisha had got ahead of him.

"Well done, Elisha!" thought he. "See how he has pushed ahead. He must have come across some one who showed him the way. When we get out I will find him, get rid of this fellow in the skull-cap, and keep to Elisha. Perhaps he will show me how to get to the front also."

Efím kept looking out, so as not to lose sight of Elisha. But when the Mass was over the crowd began to sway, pushing forward to kiss the tomb, and pushed Efím aside. He was again seized with fear lest his purse should be stolen. Pressing it with his hand, he began elbowing through the crowd, anxious only to get out. When he reached the open he went about for a long time searching for Elisha both outside and in the Church itself. In the chapels of the Church he saw many people of all kinds, eating, and drinking wine, and reading and sleeping there. But Elisha was nowhere to be seen. So Efím returned to the inn without having found his comrade. That evening the pilgrim in the skull-cap did not turn up. He had gone off without re-paying the rúble, and Efím was left alone.

The next day Efím went to the Holy Sepulchre again, with an old man from Tambóv, whom he had met on the ship. He tried to get to the front, but was again pressed back; so he stood by a pillar and prayed. He looked before him, and there in the

120

foremost place under the lamps, close to the very Sepulchre of the Lord, stood Elisha, with his arms spread out like a priest at the altar, and with his bald head all shining.

"Well, now," thought Efím, "I won't lose him!"

He pushed forward to the front, but when he got there, there was no Elisha: he had evidently gone away.

Again on the third day Efím looked, and saw at the Sepulchre, in the holiest place, Elisha standing in the sight of all men, his arms outspread and his eyes gazing upwards as if he saw something above. And his bald head was all shining.

"Well, this time," thought Efím, "he shall not escape me! I will go and stand at the door, then we can't miss one another!"

Efím went out and stood by the door till past noon. Every one had passed out, but still Elisha did not appear.

Efím remained six weeks in Jerusalem, and went everywhere: to Bethlehem, and to Bethany, and to the Jordan. He had a new shroud stamped at the Holy Sepulchre for his burial, and he took a bottle of water from the Jordan and some holy earth, and bought candles that had been lit at the sacred flame. In eight places he inscribed names to be prayed for, and he spent all his money except just enough to get home with. Then he started homeward. He walked to Jaffa, sailed thence to Odessa, and walked home from there on foot.

X I

Efím traveled the same road he had come by; and as he drew nearer home his former anxiety returned as to how affairs were getting on in his absence. "Much water flows away in a year," the proverb says. It takes a lifetime to build up a homestead but not long to ruin it, thought he. And he wondered how his son had managed without him, what sort of spring they were having, how the cattle had wintered, and whether the cottage was well finished. When Efím came to the district where he had parted from Elisha the summer before, he could hardly believe that the people living there were the same. The year before they had been starving, but now they were living in comfort. The harvest had been good, and the people had recovered and had forgotten their former misery.

One evening Efím reached the very place where Elisha had remained behind; and as he entered the village a little girl in a white smock ran out of a hut.

"Daddy, daddy, come to our house!"

Efím meant to pass on, but the little girl would not let him. She took hold of his coat, laughing, and pulled him towards the hut, where a woman with a small boy came out into the porch and beckoned to him.

"Come in, grandfather," she said. "Have supper and spend the night with us."

So Efím went in.

"I may as well ask about Elisha," he thought. "I fancy this is the very hut he went to for a drink of water."

The woman helped him off with the bag he carried, and gave him water to wash his face. Then she made him sit down to table, and set milk, curd-cakes, and porridge, before him. Efím thanked her, and praised her for her kindness to a pilgrim. The woman shook her head.

"We have good reason to welcome pilgrims," she said. "It was a pilgrim who showed us what life is. We were living forgetful of God and God punished us almost to death. We reached such a pass last summer that we all lay ill and helpless with nothing to eat. And we should have died, but that God sent an old man to help us—just such a one as you. He came in one day to ask for a drink of water, saw the state we were in, took pity on us, and remained with us. He gave us food and drink

122

and set us on our feet again; and he redeemed our land, and bought a cart and horse and gave them to us."

Here the old woman, entering the hut, interrupted the younger one and said:

"We don't know whether it was a man or an angel from God. He loved us all, pitied us all, and went away without telling us his name, so that we don't even know whom to pray for. I can see it all before me now! There I lay waiting for death, when in comes a bald-headed old man. He was not anything much to look at, and he asked for a drink of water. I, sinner that I am, thought to myself: 'What does he come prowling about here for?' And just think what he did! As soon as he saw us he let down his bag, on this very spot, and untied it."

Here the little girl joined in.

"No, Granny," said she, "first he put it down here in the middle of the hut, and then he lifted it on to the bench."

And they began discussing and recalling all he had said and done, where he sat and slept, and what he had said to each of them.

At night the peasant himself came home on his horse, and he too began to tell about Elisha and how he had lived with them.

"Had he not come we should all have died in our sins. We were dying in despair, murmuring against God and man. But he set us on our feet again; and through him we learned to know God and to believe that there is good in man. May the Lord bless him! We used to live like animals, he made human beings of us."

After giving Efím food and drink, they showed him where he was to sleep; and lay down to sleep themselves.

But though Efím lay down, he could not sleep. He could not get Elisha out of his mind, but remembered how he had seen him three times at Jerusalem, standing in the foremost place.

123

"So that is how he got ahead of me," thought Efím. "God may or may not have accepted my pilgrimage, but He has certainly accepted his!"

Next morning Efím bade farewell to the people, who put some patties in his sack before they went to their work, and he continued his journey.

XII

Efím had been away just a year and it was spring again when he reached home one evening. His son was not at home, but had gone to the public-house, and when he came back he had had a drop too much. Efím began questioning him. Everything showed that the young fellow had been unsteady during his father's absence. The money had all been wrongly spent and the work had been neglected. The father began to upbraid the son, and the son answered rudely.

"Why didn't you stay and look after it yourself?" he said. "You go off, taking the money with you, and now you demand it of me!"

The old man grew angry and struck his son.

In the morning Efím went to the village elder to complain of his son's conduct. As he was passing Elisha's house his friend's wife greeted him from the porch.

"How do you do, neighbor?" she said. "How do you do, dear friend? Did you get to Jerusalem safely?"

Efím stopped.

"Yes, thank God," he said. "I have been there. I lost sight of your old man, but I hear he got home safely."

The old woman was fond of talking:

"Yes, neighbor, he has come back," said she. "He's been back a long time. Soon after Assumption, I think it was, he returned. And we were glad the Lord had sent him back to us!

124

We were dull without him. We can't expect much work from him any more, his years for work are past; but still he is the head of the household and it's more cheerful when he's at home. And how glad our lad was! He said, 'It's like being without sunlight, when father's away!' It was dull without him, dear friend. We're fond of him, and take good care of him."

"Is he at home now?"

"He is, dear friend. He is with his bees. He is hiving the swarms. He says they are swarming well this year. The Lord has given such strength to the bees that my husband doesn't remember the like. 'The Lord is not rewarding us according to our sins,' he says. Come in, dear neighbor, he will be so glad to see you again."

Efím passed through the passage into the yard and to the apiary, to see Elisha. There was Elisha in his grey coat, without any face-net or gloves, standing under the birch trees, looking upwards, his arms stretched out and his bald head shining as Efím had seen him at the Holy Sepulchre in Jerusalem; and above him the sunlight shone through the birches as the flames of fire had done in the Holy Place, and the golden bees flew round his head like a halo, and did not sting him.

Efím stopped. The old woman called to her husband.

"Here's your friend come," she cried.

Elisha looked round with a pleased face, and came towards Efím, gently picking bees out of his own beard.

"Good-day, neighbor, good-day, dear friend. Did you get there safely?"

"My feet walked there and I have brought you some water from the river Jordan. You must come to my house for it. But whether the Lord accepted my efforts. . . ."

"Well, the Lord be thanked! May Christ bless you!" said Elisha.

Efím was silent for a while, and then added:

125

"My feet have been there, but whether my soul or another's has been there more truly . . ."

"That's God's business, neighbor, God's business," interrupted Elisha.

"On my return journey I stopped at the hut where you remained behind. . . ."

Elisha was alarmed, and said hurriedly:

"God's business, neighbor, God's business! Come into the cottage, I'll give you some of our honey." And Elisha changed the conversation, and talked of home affairs.

Efím sighed, and did not speak to Elisha of the people in the hut, nor of how he had seen him in Jerusalem. But he now understood that the best way to keep one's vows to God and to do His will, is for each man while he lives to show love and do good to others.

1885.

God Sees the
Truth, But Waits

IN the town of Vladímir lived a young merchant named
Iván Dmítrich Aksënov. He had two shops and a house of
his own.

Aksënov was a handsome, fair-haired, curly-headed fellow,

full of fun and very fond of singing. When quite a young man he had been given to drink and was riotous when he had had too much; but after he married he gave up drinking except now and then.

One summer Aksënov was going to the Nízhny Fair, and as he bade good-bye to his family his wife said to him, "Iván Dmítrich, do not start to-day; I have had a bad dream about you."

Aksënov laughed, and said, "You are afraid that when I get to the fair I shall go on the spree."

His wife replied: "I do not know what I am afraid of; all I know is that I had a bad dream. I dreamt you returned from the town, and when you took off your cap I saw that your hair was quite grey."

Aksënov laughed. "That's a lucky sign," said he. "See if I don't sell out all my goods and bring you some presents from the fair."

So he said good-bye to his family and drove away.

When he had travelled half-way, he met a merchant whom he knew, and they put up at the same inn for the night. They had some tea together, and then went to bed in adjoining rooms.

It was not Aksënov's habit to sleep late, and, wishing to travel while it was still cool, he aroused his driver before dawn and told him to put in the horses.

Then he made his way across to the landlord of the inn (who lived in a cottage at the back), paid his bill, and continued his journey.

When he had gone about twenty-five miles he stopped for the horses to be fed. Aksënov rested awhile in the passage of the inn, then he stepped out into the porch and, ordering a samovár to be heated, got out his guitar and began to play.

Suddenly a *tróyka*[1] drove up with tinkling bells and an official

[1] A three-horse conveyance.

alighted, followed by two soldiers. He came to Aksënov and began to question him, asking him who he was and whence he came. Aksënov answered him fully, and said, "Won't you have some tea with me?" But the official went on cross-questioning him and asking him, "Where did you spend last night? Were you alone, or with a fellow-merchant? Did you see the other merchant this morning? Why did you leave the inn before dawn?"

Aksënov wondered why he was asked all these questions, but he described all that had happened, and then added, "Why do you cross-question me as if I were a thief or a robber? I am travelling on business of my own, and there is no need to question me."

Then the official, calling the soldiers, said, "I am the police-officer of this district, and I question you because the merchant with whom you spent last night has been found with his throat cut. We must search your things."

They entered the house. The soldiers and the police-officer unstrapped Aksënov's luggage and searched it. Suddenly the officer drew a knife out of a bag, crying, "Whose knife is this?"

Aksënov looked, and seeing a blood-stained knife taken from his bag, he was frightened.

"How is it there is blood on this knife?"

Aksënov tried to answer, but could hardly utter a word, and only stammered: "I—don't know—not mine."

Then the police-officer said, "This morning the merchant was found in bed with his throat cut. You are the only person who could have done it. The house was locked from inside, and no one else was there. Here is this blood-stained knife in your bag, and your face and manner betray you! Tell me how you killed him and how much money you stole!"

Aksënov swore he had not done it; that he had not seen the merchant after they had had tea together; that he had no money except eight thousand rúbles of his own, and that the knife

131

was not his. But his voice was broken, his face pale, and he trembled with fear as though he were guilty.

The police-officer ordered the soldiers to bind Aksënov and to put him in the cart. As they tied his feet together and flung him into the cart, Aksënov crossed himself and wept. His money and goods were taken from him, and he was sent to the nearest town and imprisoned there. Inquiries as to his character were made in Vladímir. The merchants and other inhabitants of that town said that in former days he used to drink and waste his time, but that he was a good man. Then the trial came on: he was charged with murdering a merchant from Ryazán and robbing him of twenty thousand rúbles.

His wife was in despair, and did not know what to believe. Her children were all quite small; one was a baby at the breast. Taking them all with her, she went to the town where her husband was in jail. At first she was not allowed to see him; but, after much begging, she obtained permission from the officials and was taken to him. When she saw her husband in prison-dress and in chains, shut up with thieves and criminals, she fell down and did not come to her senses for a long time. Then she drew her children to her, and sat down near him. She told him of things at home, and asked about what had happened to him. He told her all, and she asked, "What can we do now?"

"We must petition the Tsar not to let an innocent man perish."

His wife told him that she had sent a petition to the Tsar, but that it had not been accepted.

Aksënov did not reply, but only looked downcast.

Then his wife said, "It was not for nothing I dreamt your hair had turned grey. You remember? You should not have started that day." And passing her fingers through his hair she said: "Ványa dearest, tell your wife the truth; was it not you who did it?"

132

"So you, too, suspect me!" said Aksënov, and, hiding his face in his hands, he began to weep. Then a soldier came to say that the wife and children must go away, and Aksënov said good-bye to his family for the last time.

When they were gone, Aksënov recalled what had been said, and when he remembered that his wife also had suspected him, he said to himself, "It seems that only God can know the truth; it is to Him alone we must appeal and from Him alone expect mercy."

And Aksënov wrote no more petitions, gave up all hope, and only prayed to God.

Aksënov was condemned to be flogged and sent to the mines. So he was flogged with a knout, and when the wounds caused by the knout were healed, he was driven to Siberia with other convicts.

For twenty-six years Aksënov lived as a convict in Siberia. His hair turned white as snow, and his beard grew long, thin, and grey. All his mirth went; he stooped; he walked slowly, spoke little, and never laughed, but he often prayed.

In prison Aksënov learnt to make boots, and earned a little money, with which he bought *The Lives of the Saints*. He read this book when it was light enough in the prison; and on Sundays in the prison-church he read the epistle and sang in the choir, for his voice was still good.

The prison authorities liked Aksënov for his meekness, and his fellow-prisoners respected him: they called him "Grandfather" and "The Saint." When they wanted to petition the prison authorities about anything, they always made Aksënov their spokesman, and when there were quarrels among the prisoners they came to him to put things right, and to judge the matter.

No news reached Aksënov from his home, and he did not even know if his wife and children were still alive.

133

One day a fresh gang of convicts came to the prison. In the evening the old prisoners collected round the new ones and asked them what towns or villages they came from, and what they were sentenced for. Among the rest Aksënov sat down near the new-comers, and listened with downcast air to what was said.

One of the new convicts, a tall, strong man of sixty, with a closely-cropped grey beard, was telling the others what he had been arrested for.

"Well, friends," he said, "I only took a horse that was tied to a sledge, and I was arrested and accused of stealing. I said I had only taken it to get home quicker, and had then let it go; besides, the driver was a personal friend of mine. So I said, 'It's all right.' 'No,' said they, 'you stole it.' But how or where I stole it they could not say. I once really did something wrong, and ought by rights to have come here long ago, but that time I was not found out. Now I have been sent here for nothing at all . . . Eh, but it's lies I'm telling you; I've been to Siberia before, but I did not stay long."

"Where are you from?" asked some one.

"From Vladímir. My family are of that town. My name is Makár, and they also call me Semënich."

Aksënov raised his head and said: "Tell me, Semënich, do you know anything of the merchants Aksënov, of Vladímir? Are they still alive?"

"Know them? Of course I do. The Aksënovs are rich, though their father is in Siberia: a sinner like ourselves, it seems! As for you, Gran'dad, how did you come here?"

Aksënov did not like to speak of his misfortune. He only sighed, and said, "For my sins I have been in prison these twenty-six years."

"What sins?" asked Makár Semënich.

But Aksënov only said, "Well, well—I must have deserved
134

it!" He would have said no more, but his companions told the new-comer how Aksënov came to be in Siberia: how some one had killed a merchant and had put a knife among Aksënov's things, and he had been unjustly condemned.

When Makár Semënich heard this he looked at Aksënov, slapped his own knee, and exclaimed, "Well, this is wonderful! Really wonderful! But how old you've grown, Gran'dad!"

The others asked him why he was so surprised, and where he had seen Aksënov before; but Makár Semënich did not reply. He only said: "It's wonderful that we should meet here, lads!"

These words made Aksënov wonder whether this man knew who had killed the merchant; so he said, "Perhaps, Semënich, you have heard of that affair, or maybe you've seen me before?"

"How could I help hearing? The world's full of rumors. But it's long ago, and I've forgotten what I heard."

"Perhaps you heard who killed the merchant?" asked Aksënov.

Makár Semënich laughed, and replied, "It must have been him in whose bag the knife was found! If some one else hid the knife there—'He's not a thief till he's caught,' as the saying is. How could any one put a knife into your bag while it was under your head? It would surely have woke you up."

When Aksënov heard these words he felt sure this was the man who had killed the merchant. He rose and went away. All that night Aksënov lay awake. He felt terribly unhappy, and all sorts of images rose in his mind. There was the image of his wife as she was when he parted from her to go to the fair. He saw her as if she were present; her face and her eyes rose before him, he heard her speak and laugh. Then he saw his children, quite little, as they were at that time: one with a little cloak on, another at his mother's breast. And then he remembered himself as he used to be—young and merry. He remembered how

135

he sat playing the guitar in the porch of the inn where he was arrested, and how free from care he had been. He saw in his mind the place where he was flogged, the executioner, and the people standing around; the chains, the convicts, all the twenty-six years of his prison life, and his premature old age. The thought of it all made him so wretched that he was ready to kill himself.

"And it's all that villain's doing!" thought Aksënov. And his anger was so great against Makár Semënich that he longed for vengeance, even if he himself should perish for it. He kept saying prayers all night, but could get no peace. During the day he did not go near Makár Semënich, nor even look at him.

A fortnight passed in this way. Aksënov could not sleep at nights and was so miserable that he did not know what to do.

One night as he was walking about the prison he noticed some earth that came rolling out from under one of the shelves on which the prisoners slept. He stopped to see what it was. Suddenly Makár Semënich crept out from under the shelf, and looked up at Aksënov with frightened face. Aksënov tried to pass without looking at him, but Makár seized his hand and told him that he had dug a hole under the wall, getting rid of the earth by putting it into his high boots and emptying it out every day on the road when the prisoners were driven to their work.

"Just you keep quiet, old man, and you shall get out too. If you blab they'll flog the life out of me, but I will kill you first."

Aksënov trembled with anger as he looked at his enemy. He drew his hand away, saying, "I have no wish to escape, and you have no need to kill me; you killed me long ago! As to telling of you—I may do so or not, as God shall direct."

Next day, when the convicts were led out to work, the convoy soldiers noticed that one or other of the prisoners emptied some earth out of his boots. The prison was searched and the tunnel

136

found. The Governor came and questioned all the prisoners to find out who had dug the hole. They all denied any knowledge of it. Those who knew would not betray Makár Semënich, knowing he would be flogged almost to death. At last the Governor turned to Aksënov, whom he knew to be a just man, and said:

"You are a truthful old man; tell me, before God, who dug the hole?"

Makár Semënich stood as if he were quite unconcerned, looking at the Governor and not so much as glancing at Aksënov. Aksënov's lips and hands trembled, and for a long time he could not utter a word. He thought, "Why should I screen him who ruined my life? Let him pay for what I have suffered. But if I tell, they will probably flog the life out of him, and maybe I suspect him wrongly. And, after all, what good would it be to me?"

"Well, old man," repeated the Governor, "tell us the truth: who has been digging under the wall?"

Aksënov glanced at Makár Semënich and said, "I cannot say, your Honor. It is not God's will that I should tell! Do what you like with me; I am in your hands."

However much the Governor tried, Aksënov would say no more, and so the matter had to be left.

That night, when Aksënov was lying on his bed and just beginning to doze, some one came quietly and sat down on his bed. He peered through the darkness and recognized Makár.

"What more do you want of me?" asked Aksënov. "Why have you come here?"

Makár Semënich was silent. So Aksënov sat up and said, "What do you want? Go away or I will call the guard!"

Makár Semënich bent close over Aksënov, and whispered, "Iván Dmítrich, forgive me!"

"What for?" asked Aksënov.

137

"It was I who killed the merchant and hid the knife among your things. I meant to kill you too, but I heard a noise outside; so I hid the knife in your bag and escaped through the window."

Aksënov was silent and did not know what to say. Makár Semënich slid off the bed-shelf and knelt upon the ground. "Iván Dmítrich," said he, "forgive me! For the love of God, forgive me! I will confess that it was I who killed the merchant, and you will be released and can go to your home."

"It is easy for you to talk," said Aksënov, "but I have suffered for you these twenty-six years. Where could I go to now? My wife is dead, and my children have forgotten me. I have nowhere to go. . . ."

Makár Semënich did not rise, but beat his head on the floor. "Iván Dmítrich, forgive me!" he cried. "When they flogged me with the knout it was not so hard to bear as it is to see you now . . . yet you had pity on me and did not tell. For Christ's sake forgive me, wretch that I am!" And he began to sob.

When Aksënov heard him sobbing he, too, began to weep.

"God will forgive you!" said he. "Maybe I am a hundred times worse than you." And at these words his heart grew light and the longing for home left him. He no longer had any desire to leave the prison, but only hoped for his last hour to come.

In spite of what Aksënov had said, Makár Semënich confessed his guilt. But when the order for his release came, Aksënov was already dead.

1872.

The Godson

"Ye have heard that it was said, An eye for an eye, and a tooth for a tooth, but I say unto you, Resist not him that is evil."—Matt. v. 38, 39.
"Vengeance is mine; I will repay."—Rom. xii. 19.

A SON was born to a poor peasant. He was glad, and went to his neighbor to ask him to stand godfather to the boy. The neighbor refused—he did not like standing godfather to a poor man's child. The peasant asked another neighbor, but he too refused, and after that the poor father went to every house in the village, but found no one willing to be godfather to his son. So he set off to another village, and on the way he met a man who stopped and said:

"Good-day, my good man; where are you off to?"

"God has given me a child," said the peasant, "to rejoice my eyes in youth, to comfort my old age, and to pray for my soul after death. But I am poor, and no one in our village will stand godfather to him, so I am now on my way to seek a godfather for him elsewhere."

"Let me be godfather," said the stranger.

The peasant was glad, and thanked him, but added:

"And whom shall I ask to be godmother?"

"Go to the town," replied the stranger, "and, in the square, you will see a stone house with shop-windows in the front. At the entrance you will find the tradesman to whom it belongs. Ask him to let his daughter stand godmother to your child."

The peasant hesitated.

"How can I ask a rich tradesman?" said he. "He will despise me, and will not let his daughter come."

"Don't trouble about that. Go and ask. Get everything ready by to-morrow morning, and I will come to the christening."

The poor peasant returned home, and then drove to the town to find the tradesman. He had hardly taken his horse into the yard, when the tradesman himself came out.

"What do you want?" said he.

"Why, sir," said the peasant, "you see God has given me a son to rejoice my eyes in youth, to comfort my old age, and to pray for my soul after death. Be so kind as to let your daughter stand godmother to him."

"And when is the christening?" said the tradesman.

"To-morrow morning."

142

"Very well. Go in peace. She shall be with you at Mass to-morrow morning."

The next day the godmother came, and the godfather also, and the infant was baptized. Immediately after the christening the godfather went away. They did not know who he was and never saw him again.

I I

The child grew up to be a joy to his parents. He was strong, willing to work, clever and obedient. When he was ten years old his parents sent him to school to learn to read and write. What others learnt in five years, he learnt in one, and soon there was nothing more they could teach him.

Easter came round, and the boy went to see his godmother, to give her his Easter greeting.

"Father and mother," said he when he got home again, "where does my godfather live? I should like to give him my Easter greeting, too."

And his father answered:

"We know nothing about your godfather, dear son. We often regret it ourselves. Since the day you were christened we have never seen him, nor had any news of him. We do not know where he lives, or even whether he is still alive."

The son bowed to his parents.

"Father and mother," said he, "let me go and look for my godfather. I must find him and give him my Easter greeting."

So his father and mother let him go, and the boy set off to find his godfather.

I I I

The boy left the house and set out along the road. He had been walking for several hours when he met a stranger who stopped him and said:

143

"Good-day to you, my boy. Where are you going?"

And the boy answered:

"I went to see my godmother and to give her my Easter greeting, and when I got home I asked my parents where my godfather lives, that I might go and greet him also. They told me they did not know. They said he went away as soon as I was christened, and they know nothing about him, not even if he be still alive. But I wished to see my godfather, and so I have set out to look for him."

Then the stranger said: "I am your godfather."

The boy was glad to hear this. After kissing his godfather three times for an Easter greeting, he asked him:

"Which way are you going now, godfather? If you are coming our way, please come to our house; but if you are going home, I will go with you."

"I have no time now," replied his godfather, "to come to your house. I have business in several villages, but I shall return home again to-morrow. Come and see me then."

"But how shall I find you, godfather?"

"When you leave home, go straight towards the rising sun, and you will come to a forest; going through the forest you will come to a glade. When you reach this glade sit down and rest awhile, and look around you and see what happens. On the further side of the forest you will find a garden, and in it a house with a golden roof. That is my home. Go up to the gate, and I will myself be there to meet you."

And having said this the godfather disappeared from his godson's sight.

IV

The boy did as his godfather had told him. He walked eastward until he reached a forest, and there he came to a glade, and in the midst of the glade he saw a pine tree to a branch of

144

which was tied a rope supporting a heavy log of oak. Close under this log stood a wooden trough filled with honey. Hardly had the boy had time to wonder why the honey was placed there and why the log hung above it, when he heard a crackling in the wood and saw some bears approaching: a she-bear, followed by a yearling and three tiny cubs. The she-bear, sniffing the air, went straight to the trough, the cubs following her. She thrust her muzzle into the honey, and called the cubs to do the same. They scampered up and began to eat. As they did so, the log, which the she-bear had moved aside with her head, swung away a little and, returning, gave the cubs a push. Seeing this the she-bear shoved the log away with her paw. It swung further out and returned more forcibly, striking one cub on the back and another on the head. The cubs ran away howling with pain, and the mother, with a growl, caught the log in her fore paws and, raising it above her head, flung it away. The log flew high in the air, and the yearling, rushing to the trough, pushed his muzzle into the honey and began to suck noisily. The others also drew near, but they had not reached the trough when the log, flying back, struck the yearling on the head and killed him. The mother growled louder than before and seizing the log, flung it from her with all her might. It flew higher than the branch it was tied to; so high that the rope slackened; and the she-bear returned to the trough, and the little cubs after her. The log flew higher and higher, then stopped, and began to fall. The nearer it came the faster it swung, and at last, at full speed, it crashed down on her head. The she-bear rolled over, her legs jerked, and she died. The cubs ran away into the forest.

V

The boy watched all this in surprise, and then continued his way. Leaving the forest, he came upon a large garden in the midst of which stood a lofty palace with a golden roof. At the gate stood his godfather, smiling. He welcomed his godson, and led him through the gateway into the garden. The boy had never dreamed of such beauty and delight as surrounded him in that place.

Then his godfather led him into the palace, which was even more beautiful inside than out. The godfather showed the boy through all the rooms: each brighter and finer than the other, but at last they came to one door that was sealed up.

"You see this door," said he. "It is not locked, but only sealed. It can be opened, but I forbid you to open it. You may live here, and go where you please, and enjoy all the delights of the place. My only command is—do not open that door! But should you ever do so, remember what you saw in the forest."

Having said this the godfather went away. The godson remained in the palace, and life there was so bright and joyful that he thought he had only been there three hours when he had really lived there thirty years. When thirty years had gone by the godson happened to be passing the sealed door one day, and he wondered why his godfather had forbidden him to enter that room.

"I'll just look in and see what is there," thought he, and he gave the door a push. The seals gave way, the door opened, and the godson entering saw a hall more lofty and beautiful than all the others, and in the midst of it a throne. He wandered about the hall for a while, and then mounted the steps and seated himself upon the throne. As he sat there he noticed a sceptre leaning against the throne, and took it in his hand. Hardly had he done so when the four walls of the hall suddenly disappeared. The godson looked around, and saw the whole world, and all that men were doing in it. He looked in front, and saw the sea with ships sailing on it. He looked to the right, and saw where strange heathen people lived. He looked to the

146

left, and saw where men who were Christians, but not Russians, lived. He looked round, and on the fourth side, he saw Russian people, like himself.

"I will look," said he, "and see what is happening at home, and whether the harvest is good."

He looked towards his father's fields and saw the sheaves standing in shocks. He began counting them to see whether there was much corn, when he noticed a peasant driving in a cart. It was night, and the godson thought it was his father coming to cart the corn by night. But as he looked he recognized Vasíli Kudryashóv, the thief, driving into the field and beginning to load the sheaves on to his cart. This made the godson angry and he called out:

"Father, the sheaves are being stolen from our field!"

His father, who was out with the horses in the night-pasture, woke up.

"I dreamt the sheaves were being stolen," said he. "I will just ride down and see."

So he got on a horse and rode out to the field. Finding Vasíli there, he called together other peasants to help him, and Vasíli was beaten, bound, and taken to prison.

Then the godson looked at the town, where his godmother lived. He saw that she was now married to a tradesman. She lay asleep, and her husband rose and went to his mistress. The godson shouted to her:

"Get up, get up, your husband has taken to evil ways."

The godmother jumped up and dressed, and finding out where her husband was, she shamed and beat his mistress, and drove him away.

Then the godson looked for his mother, and saw her lying asleep in her cottage. And a thief crept into the cottage and began to break open the chest in which she kept her things.

147

The mother awoke and screamed, and the robber, seizing an axe, swung it over his head to kill her.

The godson could not refrain from hurling the sceptre at the robber. It struck him upon the temple, and killed him on the spot.

VI

As soon as the godson had killed the robber, the walls closed and the hall became just as it had been before.

Then the door opened and the godfather entered, and coming up to his godson he took him by the hand and led him down from the throne.

"You have not obeyed my command," said he. "You did one wrong thing when you opened the forbidden door; another, when you mounted the throne and took my sceptre into your hands; and you have now done a third wrong, which has much increased the evil in the world. Had you sat here an hour longer, you would have ruined half mankind."

Then the godfather led his godson back to the throne, and took the sceptre in his hand; and again the walls fell asunder and all things became visible. And the godfather said:

"See what you have done to your father. Vasíli has now been a year in prison, and has come out having learnt every kind of wickedness, and has become quite incorrigible. See, he has stolen two of your father's horses, and he is now setting fire to his barn. All this you have brought upon your father."

The godson saw his father's barn breaking into flames, but his godfather shut off the sight from him, and told him to look another way.

"Here is your godmother's husband," he said. "It is a year since he left his wife, and now he goes after other women. His former mistress has sunk to still lower depths. Sorrow has

148

driven his wife to drink. That's what you have done to your godmother."

The godfather shut off this also, and showed the godson his father's house. There he saw his mother weeping for her sins, repenting, and saying:

"It would have been better had the robber killed me that night. I should not have sinned so heavily."

"That," said the godfather, "is what you have done to your mother."

He shut this off also, and pointed downwards; and the godson saw two wardens holding the robber in front of a prison-house.

And the godfather said:

"This man had murdered ten men. He should have expiated his sins himself, but by killing him you have taken his sins on yourself. Now you must answer for all his sins. That is what you have done to yourself. The she-bear pushed the log aside once, and disturbed her cubs; she pushed it again, and killed her yearling; she pushed it a third time, and was killed herself. You have done the same. Now I give you thirty years to go into the world and atone for the robber's sins. If you do not atone for them, you will have to take his place."

"How am I to atone for his sins?" asked the godson.

And the godfather answered:

"When you have rid the world of as much evil as you have brought into it, you will have atoned both for your own sins and for those of the robber."

"How can I destroy evil in the world?" the godson asked.

"Go out," replied the godfather, "and walk straight towards the rising sun. After a time you will come to a field with some men in it. Notice what they are doing, and teach them what you know. Then go on and note what you see. On the fourth day you will come to a forest. In the midst of the forest is a cell,

149

and in the cell lives a hermit. Tell him all that has happened. He will teach you what to do. When you have done all he tells you, you will have atoned for your own and the robber's sins."

And, having said this, the godfather led his godson out of the gate.

VII

The godson went his way, and as he went he thought:

"How am I to destroy evil in the world? Evil is destroyed by banishing evil men, keeping them in prison, or putting them to death. How then am I to destroy evil without taking the sins of others upon myself?"

The godson pondered over it for a long time, but could come to no conclusion. He went on until he came to a field where corn was growing thick and good and ready for the reapers. The godson saw that a little calf had got in among the corn. Some men who were at hand saw it, and mounting their horses they chased it backwards and forwards through the corn. Each time the calf was about to come out of the corn, some one rode up and the calf got frightened and turned back again, and they all galloped after it, trampling down the corn. On the road stood a woman crying.

"They will chase my calf to death," she said.

And the godson said to the peasants:

"What are you doing? Come out of the cornfield, all of you, and let the woman call her calf."

The men did so; and the woman came to the edge of the cornfield and called to the calf. "Come along, browny, come along," said she. The calf pricked up its ears, listened awhile, and then ran towards the woman of its own accord, and hid its head in her skirts, almost knocking her over. The men were glad, the woman was glad, and so was the little calf.

The godson went on, and he thought:

150

"Now I see that evil spreads evil. The more people try to drive away evil, the more the evil grows. Evil, it seems, cannot be destroyed by evil; but in what way it can be destroyed, I do not know. The calf obeyed its mistress and so all went well; but if it had not obeyed her, how could we have got it out of the field?"

The godson pondered again, but came to no conclusion, and continued his way.

VIII

He went on until he came to a village. At the furthest end he stopped and asked leave to stay the night. The woman of the house was there alone, house-cleaning, and she let him in. The godson entered, and taking his seat upon the brick oven he watched what the woman was doing. He saw her finish scrubbing the room and begin scrubbing the table. Having done this, she began wiping the table with a dirty cloth. She wiped it from side to side—but it did not come clean. The soiled cloth left streaks of dirt. Then she wiped it the other way. The first streaks disappeared, but others came in their place. Then she wiped it from one end to the other, but again the same thing happened. The soiled cloth messed the table; when one streak was wiped off another was left on. The godson watched for a while in silence, and then said:

"What are you doing, mistress?"

"Don't you see I'm cleaning up for the holiday. Only I can't manage this table, it won't come clean. I'm quite tired out."

"You should rinse your cloth," said the godson, "before you wipe the table with it."

The woman did so, and soon had the table clean.

"Thank you for telling me," said she.

In the morning he took leave of the woman and went on his way. After walking a good while, he came to the edge of a forest.

151

There he saw some peasants who were making wheel-rims of bent wood. Coming nearer, the godson saw that the men were going round and round, but could not bend the wood.

He stood and looked on, and noticed that the block, to which the piece of wood was fastened, was not fixed, but as the men moved round it went round too. Then the godson said:

"What are you doing, friends?"

"Why, don't you see, we are making wheel-rims. We have twice steamed the wood, and are quite tired out, but the wood will not bend."

"You should fix the block, friends," said the godson, "or else it goes round when you do."

The peasants took his advice and fixed the block, and then the work went on merrily.

The godson spent the night with them, and then went on. He walked all day and all night, and just before dawn he came upon some drovers encamped for the night, and lay down beside them. He saw that they had got all their cattle settled, and were trying to light a fire. They had taken dry twigs and lighted them, but before the twigs had time to burn up, they smothered them with damp brushwood. The brushwood hissed, and the fire smouldered and went out. Then the drovers brought more dry wood, lit it, and again put on the brushwood—and again the fire went out. They struggled with it for a long time, but could not get the fire to burn. Then the godson said:

"Do not be in such a hurry to put on the brushwood. Let the dry wood burn up properly before you put any on. When the fire is well alight you can put on as much as you please."

The drovers followed his advice. They let the fire burn up fiercely before adding the brushwood, which then flared up so that they soon had a roaring fire.

The godson remained with them for a while and then con-

tinued his way. He went on, wondering what the three things
he had seen might mean; but he could not fathom them.

IX

The godson walked the whole of that day, and in the evening
came to another forest. There he found a hermit's cell, at which
he knocked.

"Who is there?" asked a voice from within.

"A great sinner," replied the godson. "I must atone for
another's sins as well as for my own."

The hermit hearing this came out.

"What sins are those that you have to bear for another?"

The godson told him everything: about his godfather; about
the she-bear with the cubs; about the throne in the sealed room;
about the commands his godfather had given him, as well as
about the peasants he had seen trampling down the corn, and
the calf that ran out when its mistress called it.

"I have seen that one cannot destroy evil by evil," said he,
"but I cannot understand how it is to be destroyed. Teach me
how it can be done."

"Tell me," replied the hermit, "what else you have seen on
your way."

The godson told him about the woman washing the table,
and the men making wheel-rims, and the drovers lighting their
fire.

The hermit listened to it all, and then went back to his cell
and brought out an old jagged axe.

"Come with me," said he.

When they had gone some way, the hermit pointed to a tree.

"Cut it down," he said.

The godson felled the tree.

"Now chop it into three," said the hermit.

153

The godson chopped the tree into three pieces. Then the hermit went back to his cell, and brought out some blazing sticks.

"Burn those three logs," said he.

So the godson made a fire, and burnt the three logs till only three charred stumps remained.

"Now plant them half in the ground, like this."

The godson did so.

"You see that river at the foot of the hill. Bring water from there in your mouth, and water these stumps. Water this stump, as you taught the woman: this one, as you taught the wheel-wrights: and this one, as you taught the drovers. When all three have taken root and from these charred stumps apple-trees have sprung, you will know how to destroy evil in men, and will have atoned for all your sins."

Having said this, the hermit returned to his cell. The godson pondered for a long time, but could not understand what the hermit meant. Nevertheless he set to work to do as he had been told.

X

The godson went down to the river, filled his mouth with water, and returning, emptied it on to one of the charred stumps. This he did again and again, and watered all three stumps. When he was hungry and quite tired out, he went to the cell to ask the old hermit for some food. He opened the door, and there upon a bench he saw the old man lying dead. The godson looked round for food, and he found some dried bread, and ate a little of it. Then he took a spade and set to work to dig the hermit's grave. During the night he carried water and watered the stumps, and in the day he dug the grave. He had hardly finished the grave, and was about to bury the corpse,

154

when some people from the village came, bringing food for the old man.

The people heard that the old hermit was dead, and that he had given the godson his blessing and left him in his place. So they buried the old man, gave the bread they had brought to the godson, and promising to bring him some more, they went away.

The godson remained in the old man's place. There he lived, eating the food people brought him, and doing as he had been told: carrying water from the river in his mouth and watering the charred stumps.

He lived thus for a year and many people visited him. His fame spread abroad, as a holy man who lived in the forest and brought water from the bottom of a hill in his mouth to water charred stumps for the salvation of his soul. People flocked to see him. Rich merchants drove up bringing him presents, but he kept only the barest necessaries for himself and gave the rest away to the poor.

And so the godson lived: carrying water in his mouth and watering the stumps half the day, and resting and receiving people the other half. And he began to think that this was the way he had been told to live in order to destroy evil and atone for his sins.

He spent two years in this manner, not omitting for a single day to water the stumps. But still not one of them sprouted.

One day, as he sat in his cell, he heard a man ride past, singing as he went. The godson came out to see what sort of a man it was. He saw a strong young fellow, well dressed, and mounted on a handsome, well-saddled horse.

The godson stopped him, and asked him who he was, and where he was going.

"I am a robber," the man answered, drawing rein. "I ride

about the highways killing people, and the more I kill, the merrier are the songs I sing."

The godson was horror-struck, and thought:

"How can the evil be destroyed in such a man as this? It is easy to speak to those who come to me of their own accord and confess their sins. But this one boasts of the evil he does."

So he said nothing and turned away, thinking: "What am I to do now? This robber may take to riding about here, and he will frighten away the people. They will leave off coming to me. It will be a loss to them, and I shall not know how to live."

So the godson turned back and said to the robber:

"People come to me here, not to boast of their sins, but to repent and to pray for forgiveness. Repent of your sins, if you fear God; but if there is no repentance in your heart, then go away and never come here again. Do not trouble me, and do not frighten people away from me. If you do not hearken, God will punish you."

The robber laughed:

"I am not afraid of God, and I will not listen to you. You are not my master," said he. "You live by your piety, and I by my robbery. We all must live. You may teach the old women who come to you, but you have nothing to teach me. And because you have reminded me of God, I will kill two more men to-morrow. I would kill you, but I do not want to soil my hands just now. See that in future you keep out of my way!"

Having uttered this threat, the robber rode away. He did not come again, and the godson lived in peace, as before, for eight more years.

XI

One night the godson watered his stumps, and, after returning to his cell, he sat down to rest, and watched the footpath, wondering if some one would soon come. But no one came at all that day. He sat alone till evening, feeling lonely and dull, and he thought about his past life. He remembered how the robber had reproached him for living by his piety; and he reflected on his way of life. "I am not living as the hermit commanded me to," thought he. "The hermit laid a penance upon me, and I have made both a living and fame out of it; and have been so tempted by it, that now I feel dull when people do not come to me; and when they do come, I only rejoice because they praise my holiness. That is not how one should live. I have been led astray by love of praise. I have not atoned for my past sins, but have added fresh ones. I will go to another part of the forest where people will not find me; and I will live so as to atone for my old sins and commit no fresh ones."

Having come to this conclusion the godson filled a bag with dried bread and, taking a spade, left the cell and started for a ravine he knew of in a lonely spot, where he could dig himself a cave and hide from the people.

As he was going along with his bag and his spade he saw the robber riding toward him. The godson was frightened and started to run away, but the robber overtook him.

"Where are you going?" asked the robber.

The godson told him he wished to get away from the people and live somewhere where no one would come to him. This surprised the robber.

"What will you live on, if people do not come to see you?" asked he.

The godson had not even thought of this, but the robber's question reminded him that food would be necessary.

"On what God pleases to give me," he replied.

The robber said nothing, and rode away.

"Why did I not say anything to him about his way of life?" thought the godson. "He might repent now. To-day he seems

157

in a gentler mood, and has not threatened to kill me." And he shouted to the robber:

"You have still to repent of your sins. You cannot escape from God."

The robber turned his horse, and drawing a knife from his girdle threatened the hermit with it. The latter was alarmed, and ran away further into the forest.

The robber did not follow him, but only shouted:

"Twice I have let you off, old man, but next time you come in my way I will kill you!"

Having said this, he rode away. In the evening when the godson went to water his stumps—one of them was sprouting! A little apple-tree was growing out of it.

XII

After hiding himself from everybody, the godson lived all alone. When his supply of bread was exhausted, he thought: "Now I must go and look for some roots to eat." He had not gone far, however, before he saw a bag of dried bread hanging on a branch. He took it down, and as long as it lasted he lived upon that.

When he had eaten it all, he found another bagful on the same branch. So he lived on, his only trouble being his fear of the robber. Whenever he heard the robber passing, he hid, thinking:

"He may kill me before I have had time to atone for my sins."

In this way he lived for ten more years. The one apple-tree continued to grow, but the other two stumps remained exactly as they were.

One morning the godson rose early and went to his work. By the time he had thoroughly moistened the ground round the stumps, he was tired out and sat down to rest. As he sat there he thought to himself:

"I have sinned, and have become afraid of death. It may be God's will that I should redeem my sins by death."

Hardly had this thought crossed his mind when he heard the robber riding up, swearing at something. When the godson heard this, he thought:

"No evil and no good can befall me from any one but from God."

And he went to meet the robber. He saw the robber was not alone, but behind him on the saddle sat another man, gagged, and bound hand and foot. The man was doing nothing, but the robber was abusing him violently. The godson went up and stood in front of the horse.

"Where are you taking this man?" he asked.

"Into the forest," replied the robber. "He is a merchant's son, and will not tell me where his father's money is hidden. I am going to flog him till he tells me."

And the robber spurred on his horse, but the godson caught hold of his bridle, and would not let him pass.

"Let this man go!" he said.

The robber grew angry, and raised his arm to strike.

"Would you like a taste of what I am going to give this man? Have I not promised to kill you? Let go!"

The godson was not afraid.

"You shall not go," said he. "I do not fear you. I fear no one but God, and He wills that I should not let you pass. Set this man free!"

The robber frowned, and snatching out his knife, cut the ropes with which the merchant's son was bound, and set him free.

"Get away, both of you," he said, "and beware how you cross my path again."

159

The merchant's son jumped down and ran away. The robber was about to ride on, but the godson stopped him again, and again spoke to him about giving up his evil life. The robber heard him to the end in silence, and then rode away without a word.

The next morning the godson went to water his stumps and lo! the second stump was sprouting. A second young apple-tree had begun to grow.

XIII

Another ten years had gone by. The godson was sitting quietly one day, desiring nothing, fearing nothing, and with a heart full of joy.

"What blessings God showers on men!" thought he. "Yet how needlessly they torment themselves. What prevents them from living happily?"

And remembering all the evil in men and the troubles they bring upon themselves, his heart filled with pity.

"It is wrong of me to live as I do." he said to himself. "I must go and teach others what I have myself learnt."

Hardly had he thought this, when he heard the robber approaching. He let him pass, thinking:

"It is no good talking to him, he will not understand."

That was his first thought, but he changed his mind and went out into the road. He saw that the robber was gloomy, and was riding with downcast eyes. The godson looked at him, pitied him, and running up to him laid his hand upon his knee.

"Brother, dear," said he, "have some pity on your own soul! In you lives the spirit of God. You suffer, and torment others, and lay up more and more suffering for the future. Yet God loves you and has prepared such blessings for you. Do not ruin yourself utterly. Change your life!"

160

The robber frowned and turned away.

"Leave me alone!" said he.

But the godson held the robber still faster, and began to weep.

Then the robber lifted his eyes and looked at the godson. He looked at him for a long time, and alighting from his horse, fell on his knees at the godson's feet.

"You have overcome me, old man," said he. "For twenty years I have resisted you, but now you have conquered me. Do what you will with me, for I have no more power over myself. When you first tried to persuade me, it only angered me more. Only when you hid yourself from men did I begin to consider your words, for I saw then that you asked nothing of them for yourself. Since that day I have brought food for you, hanging it upon the tree."

Then the godson remembered that the woman got her table clean only after she had rinsed her cloth. In the same way, it was only when he ceased caring about himself, and cleansed his own heart, that he was able to cleanse the hearts of others.

The robber went on.

"When I saw that you did not fear death, my heart turned."

Then the godson remembered that the wheelwrights could not bend the rims until they had fixed their block. So, not till he had cast away the fear of death and made his life fast in God, could he subdue this man's unruly heart.

"But my heart did not quite melt," continued the robber, "until you pitied me and wept for me."

The godson, full of joy, led the robber to the place where the stumps were. And when they got there, they saw that from the third stump an apple-tree had begun to sprout. And the godson remembered that the drovers had not been able to light the damp wood until the fire had burnt up well. So it was only when his own heart burnt warmly, that another's heart had been kindled by it.

161

And the godson was full of joy that he had at last atoned for his sins.

He told all this to the robber, and died. The robber buried him, and lived as the godson had commanded him, teaching to others what the godson had taught him.

1886.

Master and Man

IT happened in the 'seventies in winter, on the day after St. Nicholas's Day. There was a fete in the parish and the innkeeper, Vasíli Andréevich Brekhunóv, a Second Guild mer-

165

chant, being a church elder had to go to church, and had also to entertain his relatives and friends at home.

But when the last of them had gone he at once began to prepare to drive over to see a neighboring proprietor about a grove which he had been bargaining over for a long time. He was now in a hurry to start, lest buyers from the town might forestall him in making a profitable purchase.

The youthful landowner was asking ten thousand rúbles for the grove simply because Vasíli Andréevich was offering seven thousand. Seven thousand was, however, only a third of its real value. Vasíli Andréevich might perhaps have got it down to his own price, for the woods were in his district and he had a long-standing agreement with the other village dealers that no one should run up the price in another's district, but he had now learnt that some timber-dealers from town meant to bid for the Goryáchkin grove, and he resolved to go at once and get the matter settled. So as soon as the feast was over, he took seven hundred rúbles from his strong box, added to them two thousand three hundred rúbles of church money he had in his keeping, so as to make up the sum to three thousand; carefully counted the notes, and having put them into his pocket-book made haste to start.

Nikíta, the only one of Vasíli Andréevich's laborers who was not drunk that day, ran to harness the horse. Nikíta, though an habitual drunkard, was not drunk that day because since the last day before the fast, when he had drunk up his coat and leather boots, he had sworn off drink and had kept his vow for two months, and was still keeping it despite the temptation of the vódka that had been drunk everywhere during the first two days of the feast.

Nikíta was a peasant of about fifty from a neighboring village, "not a manager" as the peasants said of him, meaning that he was not the thrifty head of a household but lived most of his time away from home as a laborer. He was valued every-

166

where for his industry, dexterity, and strength at work, and still more for his kindly and pleasant temper. But he never settled down anywhere for long, because about twice a year, or even oftener, he had a drinking bout, and then besides spending all his clothes on drink he became turbulent and quarrelsome. Vasíli Andréevich himself had turned him away several times, but had afterwards taken him back again—valuing his honesty, his kindness to animals, and especially his cheapness. Vasíli Andréevich did not pay Nikíta the eighty rúbles a year such a man was worth, but only about forty, which he gave him haphazard, in small sums, and even that mostly not in cash but in goods from his own shop and at high prices.

Nikíta's wife Martha, who had once been a handsome vigorous woman, managed the homestead with the help of her son and two daughters, and did not urge Nikíta to live at home: first because she had been living for some twenty years already with a cooper, a peasant from another village who lodged in their house; and second because though she managed her husband as she pleased when he was sober, she feared him like fire when he was drunk. Once when he had got drunk at home, Nikíta, probably to make up for his submissiveness when sober, broke open her box, took out her best clothes, snatched up an axe, and chopped all her under-garments and dresses to bits. All the wages Nikíta earned went to his wife, and he raised no objection to that. So now, two days before the holiday, Martha had been twice to see Vasíli Andréevich and had got from him wheat flour, tea, sugar, and a quart of vódka, the lot costing three rúbles, and also five rúbles in cash, for which she thanked him as for a special favor, though he owed Nikíta at least twenty rúbles.

"What agreement did we ever draw up with you?" said Vasíli Andréevich to Nikíta: "If you need anything, take it; you will work it off. I'm not like others to keep you waiting, and making up accounts and reckoning fines. We deal straightforwardly. You serve me and I don't neglect you."

And when saying this Vasíli Andréevich was honestly convinced that he was Nikíta's benefactor, and he knew how to put it so plausibly that all those who depended on him for their money, beginning with Nikíta, confirmed him in the conviction that he was their benefactor and did not overreach them.

"Yes, I understand, Vasíli Andréevich. You know that I serve you and take as much pains as I would for my own father. I understand very well!" Nikíta would reply. He was quite aware that Vasíli Andréevich was cheating him, but at the same time he felt that it was useless to try to clear up his accounts with him or explain his side of the matter, and that as long as he had nowhere else to go he must accept what he could get.

Now, having heard his master's order to harness, he went as usual cheerfully and willingly to the shed, stepping briskly and easily on his rather turned-in feet; took down from a nail the heavy tasselled leather bridle, and jingling the rings of the bit went to the closed stable where the horse he was to harness was standing by himself.

"What, feeling lonely, feeling lonely, little silly?" said Nikíta in answer to the low whinny with which he was greeted by the good-tempered, medium-sized bay stallion, with a rather slanting crupper, who stood alone in the shed. "Now then, now then, there's time enough. Let me water you first," he went on, speaking to the horse just as to someone who understood the words he was using, and having whisked the dusty grooved back of the well-fed young stallion with the skirt of his coat, he put a bridle on his handsome head, straightened his ears and forelock, and having taken off his halter led him out to water.

Picking his way out of the dung-strewn stable, Mukhórty frisked, and making play with his hind leg pretended that he meant to kick Nikíta, who was running at a trot beside him to the pump.

"Now then, now then, you rascal!" Nikíta called out, well knowing how carefully Mukhórty threw out his hind leg just to touch his greasy sheepskin coat but not to strike him—a trick Nikíta much appreciated.

After a drink of the cold water the horse sighed, moving his strong wet lips, from the hairs of which transparent drops fell into the trough; then standing still as if in thought, he suddenly gave a loud snort.

"If you don't want any more, you needn't. But don't go asking for any later," said Nikíta quite seriously and fully explaining his conduct to Mukhórty. Then he ran back to the shed pulling the playful young horse, who wanted to gambol all over the yard, by the rein.

There was no one else in the yard except a stranger, the cook's husband, who had come for the holiday.

"Go and ask which sledge is to be harnessed—the wide one or the small one—there's a good fellow!"

The cook's husband went into the house, which stood on an iron foundation and was iron-roofed, and soon returned saying that the little one was to be harnessed. By that time Nikíta had put the collar and brass-studded belly-band on Mukhórty and, carrying a light, painted shaft-bow in one hand, was leading the horse with the other up to two sledges that stood in the shed.

"All right, let it be the little one!" he said, backing the intelligent horse, which all the time kept pretending to bite him, into the shafts, and with the aid of the cook's husband he proceeded to harness. When everything was nearly ready and only the reins had to be adjusted, Nikíta sent the other man to the shed for some straw and to the barn for a drugget.

"There, that's all right! Now, now, don't bristle up!" said

Nikíta, pressing down into the sledge the freshly threshed oat straw the cook's husband had brought. "And now let's spread the sacking like this, and the drugget over it. There, like that it will be comfortable sitting," he went on, suiting the action to the words and tucking the drugget all round over the straw to make a seat.

"Thank you, dear man. Things always go quicker with two working at it!" he added. And gathering up the leather reins fastened together by a brass ring, Nikíta took the driver's seat and started the impatient horse over the frozen manure which lay in the yard, towards the gate.

"Uncle Nikíta! I say, Uncle, Uncle!" a high-pitched voice shouted, and a seven-year-old boy in a black sheepskin coat, new white felt boots, and a warm cap, ran hurriedly out of the house into the yard. "Take me with you!" he cried, fastening up his coat as he ran.

"All right, come along, darling!" said Nikíta, and stopping the sledge he picked up the master's pale thin little son, radiant with joy, and drove out into the road.

It was past two o'clock and the day was windy, dull, and cold, with more than twenty degrees Fahrenheit of frost. Half the sky was hidden by a lowering dark cloud. In the yard it was quiet, but in the street the wind was felt more keenly. The snow swept down from a neighboring shed and whirled about in the corner near the bath-house.

Hardly had Nikíta driven out of the yard and turned the horse's head to the house, before Vasíli Andréevich emerged from the high porch in front of the house with a cigarette in his mouth and wearing a cloth-covered sheepskin coat tightly girdled low at his waist, stepped onto the hard-trodden snow which squeaked under the leather soles of his felt boots, and stopped. Taking a last whiff of his cigarette he threw it down, stepped on it, and letting the smoke escape through his

170

moustache and looking askance at the horse that was coming up, began to tuck in his sheepskin collar on both sides of his ruddy face, clean-shaven except for the moustache, so that his breath should not moisten the collar.

"See now! The young scamp is there already!" he exclaimed when he saw his little son in the sledge. Vasíli Andréevich was excited by the vódka he had drunk with his visitors, and so he was even more pleased than usual with everything that was his and all that he did. The sight of his son, whom he always thought of as his heir, now gave him great satisfaction. He looked at him, screwing up his eyes and showing his long teeth.

His wife—pregnant, thin and pale, with her head and shoulders wrapped in a shawl so that nothing of her face could be seen but her eyes—stood behind him in the vestibule to see him off.

"Now really, you ought to take Nikíta with you," she said timidly, stepping out from the doorway.

Vasíli Andréevich did not answer. Her words evidently annoyed him and he frowned angrily and spat.

"You have money on you," she continued in the same plaintive voice. "What if the weather gets worse! Do take him, for goodness' sake!"

"Why? Don't I know the road that I must needs take a guide?" exclaimed Vasíli Andréevich, uttering every word very distinctly and compressing his lips unnaturally, as he usually did when speaking to buyers and sellers.

"Really you ought to take him. I beg you in God's name!" his wife repeated, wrapping her shawl more closely round her head.

"There, she sticks to it like a leech! . . . Where am I to take him?"

"I'm quite ready to go with you, Vasíli Andréevich," said

171

Nikíta cheerfully. "But they must feed the horses while I am away," he added, turning to his master's wife.

"I'll look after them, Nikíta dear. I'll tell Simon," replied the mistress.

"Well, Vasíli Andréevich, am I to come with you?" said Nikíta, awaiting a decision.

"It seems I must humor my old woman. But if you're coming you'd better put on a warmer cloak," said Vasíli Andréevich, smiling again as he winked at Nikíta's short sheepskin coat, which was torn under the arms and at the back, was greasy and out of shape, frayed to a fringe round the skirt, and had endured many things in its lifetime.

"Hey, dear man, come and hold the horse!" shouted Nikíta to the cook's husband, who was still in the yard.

"No, I will myself, I will myself!" shrieked the little boy, pulling his hands, red with cold, out of his pockets, and seizing the cold leather reins.

"Only don't be too long dressing yourself up. Look alive!" shouted Vasíli Andréevich, grinning at Nikíta.

"Only a moment, father, Vasíli Andréevich!" replied Nikíta, and running quickly with his inturned toes in his felt boots with their soles patched with felt, he hurried across the yard and into the workmen's hut.

"Arínushka! Get my coat down from the stove. I'm going with the master," he said, as he ran into the hut and took down his girdle from the nail on which it hung.

The workmen's cook, who had had a sleep after dinner and was now getting the samovár ready for her husband, turned cheerfully to Nikíta, and infected by his hurry began to move as quickly as he did, got down his miserable worn-out cloth coat from the stove where it was drying, and began hurriedly shaking it out and smoothing it down.

"There now, you'll have a chance of a holiday with your

goodman," said Nikíta, who from kind-hearted politeness always said something to anyone he was alone with.

Then, drawing his worn narrow girdle round him, he drew in his breath, pulling in his lean stomach still more, and girdled himself as tightly as he could over his sheepskin.

"There now," he said, addressing himself no longer to the cook but to the girdle, as he tucked the ends in at the waist, "now you won't come undone!" And working his shoulders up and down to free his arms, he put the coat over his sheepskin, arched his back more strongly to ease his arms, poked himself under the armpits, and took down his leather-covered mittens from the shelf. "Now we're all right!"

"You ought to wrap your feet up, Nikíta. Your boots are very bad."

Nikíta stopped as if he had suddenly realized this.

"Yes, I ought to. . . . But they'll do like this. It isn't far!" and he ran out into the yard.

"Won't you be cold, Nikíta?" said the mistress as he came up to the sledge.

"Cold? No, I'm quite warm," answered Nikíta as he pushed some straw up to the forepart of the sledge so that it should cover his feet, and stowed away the whip, which the good horse would not need, at the bottom of the sledge.

Vasíli Andréevich, who was wearing two fur-lined coats one over the other, was already in the sledge, his broad back filling nearly its whole rounded width, and taking the reins he immediately touched the horse. Nikíta jumped in just as the sledge started, and seated himself in front on the left side, with one leg hanging over the edge.

The good stallion took the sledge along at a brisk pace over the smooth-frozen road through the village, the runners squeaking slightly as they went.

"Look at him hanging on there! Hand me the whip, Nikíta!" shouted Vasíli Andréevich, evidently enjoying the sight of his heir, who standing on the runners was hanging on at the back of the sledge. "I'll give it you! Be off to mamma, you pup!"

The boy jumped down. The horse increased his amble and, suddenly changing foot, broke into a fast trot.

Krestý, the village where Vasíli Andréevich lived, consisted of six houses. As soon as they had passed the blacksmith's hut, the last in the village, they realized that the wind was much stronger than they had thought. The road could hardly be seen. The tracks left by the sledge-runners were immediately covered by snow and the road was only distinguished by the fact that it was higher than the rest of the ground. There was a whirl of snow over the fields and the line where sky and earth met could not be seen. The Telyátin forest, usually clearly visible, now only loomed up occasionally and dimly through the driving snowy dust. The wind came from the left, insistently blowing over to one side the mane on Mukhórty's sleek neck and carrying aside even his fluffy tail, which was tied in a simple knot. Nikíta's wide coat-collar, as he sat on the windy side, pressed close to his cheek and nose.

"This road doesn't give him a chance—it's too snowy," said Vasíli Andréevich, who prided himself on his good horse. "I once drove to Pashútino with him in half an hour."

"What?" asked Nikíta, who could not hear on account of his collar.

174

"I say I once went to Pashútino in half an hour," shouted Vasíli Andréevich.

"It goes without saying that he's a good horse," replied Nikíta.

They were silent for awhile. But Vasíli Andréevich wished to talk.

"Well, did you tell your wife not to give the cooper any vódka?" he began in the same loud tone, quite convinced that Nikíta must feel flattered to be talking with so clever and important a person as himself, and he was so pleased with his jest that it did not enter his head that the remark might be unpleasant to Nikíta.

The wind again prevented Nikíta's hearing his master's words.

Vasíli Andréevich repeated the jest about the cooper in his loud, clear voice.

"That's their business, Vasíli Andréevich. I don't pry into their affairs. As long as she doesn't ill-treat our boy—God be with them."

"That's so," said Vasíli Andréevich. "Well, and will you be buying a horse in spring?" he went on, changing the subject.

"Yes, I can't avoid it," answered Nikíta, turning down his collar and leaning back towards his master.

The conversation now became interesting to him and he did not wish to lose a word.

"The lad's growing up. He must begin to plough for himself, but till now we've always had to hire someone," he said.

"Well, why not have the lean-cruppered one. I won't charge much for it," shouted Vasíli Andréevich, feeling animated, and consequently starting on his favorite occupation—that of horse-dealing—which absorbed all his mental powers.

"Or you might let me have fifteen rúbles and I'll buy one at the horse-market," said Nikíta, who knew that the horse

175

Vasíli Andréevich wanted to sell him would be dear at seven rúbles, but that if he took it from him it would be charged at twenty-five, and then he would be unable to draw any money for half a year.

"It's a good horse. I think of your interest as of my own—according to conscience. Brekhunóv isn't a man to wrong anyone. Let the loss be mine. I'm not like others. Honestly!" he shouted in the voice in which he hypnotized his customers and dealers. "It's a real good horse."

"Quite so!" said Nikíta with a sigh, and convinced that there was nothing more to listen to, he again released his collar, which immediately covered his ear and face.

They drove on in silence for about half an hour. The wind blew sharply onto Nikíta's side and arm where his sheepskin was torn.

He huddled up and breathed into the collar which covered his mouth, and was not wholly cold.

"What do you think—shall we go through Karamýshevo or by the straight road?" asked Vasíli Andréevich.

The road through Karamýshevo was more frequented and was well marked with a double row of high stakes. The straight road was nearer but little used and had no stakes, or only poor ones covered with snow.

Nikíta thought awhile.

"Though Karamýshevo is farther, it is better going," he said.

"But by the straight road, when once we get through the hollow by the forest, it's good going—sheltered," said Vasíli Andréevich, who wished to go the nearest way.

"Just as you please," said Nikíta, and again let go of his collar.

Vasíli Andréevich did as he had said, and having gone about half a verst came to a tall oak stake which had a few dry leaves still dangling on it, and there he turned to the left.

176

On turning they faced directly against the wind, and snow was beginning to fall. Vasíli Andréevich, who was driving, inflated his cheeks, blowing the breath out through his moustache. Nikíta dozed.

So they went on in silence for about ten minutes. Suddenly Vasíli Andréevich began saying something.

"Eh, what?" asked Nikíta, opening his eyes.

Vasíli Andréevich did not answer, but bent over, looking behind them and then ahead of the horse. The sweat had curled Mukhórty's coat between his legs and on his neck. He went at a walk.

"What is it?" Nikíta asked again.

"What is it? What is it?" Vasíli Andréevich mimicked him angrily. "There are no stakes to be seen! We must have got off the road!"

"Well, pull up then, and I'll look for it," said Nikíta, and jumping down lightly from the sledge and taking the whip from under the straw, he went off to the left from his own side of the sledge.

The snow was not deep that year, so that it was possible to walk anywhere, but still in places it was knee-deep and got into Nikíta's boots. He went about feeling the ground with his feet and the whip, but could not find the road anywhere.

"Well, how is it?" asked Vasíli Andréevich when Nikíta came back to the sledge.

"There is no road this side. I must go to the other side and try there," said Nikíta.

"There's something there in front. Go and have a look."

Nikíta went to what had appeared dark, but found that it was earth which the wind had blown from the bare fields of winter oats and had strewn over the snow, coloring it. Having searched to the right also, he returned to the sledge, brushed the snow from his coat, shook it out of his boots, and seated himself once more.

"We must go to the right," he said decidedly. "The wind was blowing on our left before, but now it is straight in my face. Drive to the right," he repeated with decision.

Vasíli Andréevich took his advice and turned to the right, but still there was no road. They went on in that direction for some time. The wind was as fierce as ever and it was snowing lightly.

"It seems, Vasíli Andréevich, that we have gone quite astray," Nikíta suddenly remarked, as if it were a pleasant thing. "What is that?" he added, pointing to some potato bines that showed up from under the snow.

Vasíli Andréevich stopped the perspiring horse, whose deep sides were heaving heavily.

"What is it?"

"Why, we are on the Zakhárov lands. See where we've got to!"

"Nonsense!" retorted Vasíli Andréevich.

"It's not nonsense, Vasíli Andréevich. It's the truth," replied Nikíta. "You can feel that the sledge is going over a potato-field, and there are the heaps of bines which have been carted here. It's the Zakhárov factory land."

"Dear me, how we have gone astray!" said Vasíli Andréevich. "What are we to do now?"

"We must go straight on, that's all. We shall come out some-where—if not at Zakhárova then at the proprietor's farm," said Nikíta.

Vasíli Andréevich agreed, and drove as Nikíta had indicated. So they went on for a considerable time. At times they came onto bare fields and the sledge-runners rattled over frozen lumps of earth. Sometimes they got onto a winter-rye field, or a fallow field on which they could see stalks of wormwood, and

178

straws sticking up through the snow and swaying in the wind; sometimes they came onto deep and even white snow, above which nothing was to be seen.

The snow was falling from above and sometimes rose from below. The horse was evidently exhausted, his hair had all curled up from sweat and was covered with hoar-frost, and he went at a walk. Suddenly he stumbled and sat down in a ditch or water-course. Vasíli Andréevich wanted to stop, but Nikíta cried to him:

"Why stop? We've got in and must get out. Hey, pet! Hey, darling! Get up, old fellow!" he shouted in a cheerful tone to the horse, jumping out of the sledge and himself getting stuck in the ditch.

The horse gave a start and quickly climbed out onto the frozen bank. It was evidently a ditch that had been dug there.

"Where are we now?" asked Vasíli Andréevich.

"We'll soon find out!" Nikíta replied. "Go on, we'll get somewhere."

"Why, this must be the Goryáchkin forest!" said Vasíli Andréevich, pointing to something dark that appeared amid the snow in front of them.

"We'll see what forest it is when we get there," said Nikíta.

He saw that beside the black thing they had noticed, dry, oblong willow-leaves were fluttering, and so he knew it was not a forest but a settlement, but he did not wish to say so. And in fact they had not gone twenty-five yards beyond the ditch before something in front of them, evidently trees, showed up black, and they heard a new and melancholy sound. Nikíta had guessed right: it was not a wood, but a row of tall willows with a few leaves still fluttering on them here and there. They had evidently been planted along the ditch round a threshing-floor. Coming up to the willows, which moaned sadly in the wind, the horse suddenly planted his forelegs above the height of the

179

sledge, drew up his hind legs also, pulling the sledge onto higher ground, and turned to the left, no longer sinking up to his knees in snow. They were back on a road.

"Well, here we are, but heaven only knows where!" said Nikíta.

The horse kept straight along the road through the drifted snow, and before they had gone another hundred yards the straight line of the dark wattle wall of a barn showed up black before them, its roof heavily covered with snow which poured down from it. After passing the barn the road turned to the wind and they drove into a snow-drift. But ahead of them was a lane with houses on either side, so evidently the snow had been blown across the road and they had to drive through the drift. And so in fact it was. Having driven through the snow they came out into a street. At the end house of the village some frozen clothes hanging on a line—shirts, one red and one white, trousers, leg-bands, and a petticoat—fluttered wildly in the wind. The white shirt in particular struggled desperately, waving its sleeves about.

"There now, either a lazy woman or a dead one has not taken her clothes down before the holiday," remarked Nikíta, looking at the fluttering shirts.

III

At the entrance to the street the wind still raged and the road was thickly covered with snow, but well within the village it was calm, warm, and cheerful. At one house a dog was barking, at another a woman, covering her head with her coat, came running from somewhere and entered the door of a hut, stopping on the threshold to have a look at the passing sledge. In the middle of the village girls could be heard singing.

180

Here in the village there seemed to be less wind and snow, and the frost was less keen.

"Why, this is Gríshkino," said Vasíli Andréevich.

"So it is," responded Nikíta

It really was Gríshkino, which meant that they had gone too far to the left and had travelled some six miles, not quite in the direction they aimed at, but towards their destination for all that. From Gríshkino to Goryáchkin was about another four miles.

In the middle of the village they almost ran into a tall man walking down the middle of the street.

"Who are you?" shouted the man, stopping the horse, and recognizing Vasíli Andréevich he immediately took hold of the shaft, went along it hand over hand till he reached the sledge, and placed himself on the driver's seat.

He was Isáy, a peasant of Vasíli Andréevich's acquaintance, and well known as the principal horse-thief in the district.

"Ah, Vasíli Andréevich! Where are you off to?" said Isáy, enveloping Nikíta in the odor of the vódka he had drunk.

"We were going to Goryáchkin."

"And look where you've got to! You should have gone through Molchánovka."

"Should have, but didn't manage it," said Vasíli Andréevich, holding in the horse.

"That's a good horse," said Isáy, with a shrewd glance at Mukhórty, and with a practised hand he tightened the loosened knot high in the horse's bushy tail.

"Are you going to stay the night?"

"No, friend. I must get on."

"Your business must be pressing. And who is this? Ah, Nikíta Stepánych!"

"Who else?" replied Nikíta. "But I say, good friend, how are we to avoid going astray again?"

"Where can you go astray here? Turn back straight down

181

the street and then when you come out keep straight on. Don't take to the left. You will come out onto the high road, and then turn to the right."

"And where do we turn off the high road? As in summer, or the winter way?" asked Nikíta.

"The winter way. As soon as you turn off you'll see some bushes, and opposite them there is a way-mark—a large oak one with branches—and that's the way."

Vasíli Andréevich turned the horse back and drove through the outskirts of the village.

"Why not stay the night?" Isáy shouted after them.

But Vasíli Andréevich did not answer and touched up the horse. Four miles of good road, two of which lay through the forest, seemed easy to manage, especially as the wind was apparently quieter and the snow had stopped.

Having driven along the trodden village street, darkened here and there by fresh manure, past the yard where the clothes hung out and where the white shirt had broken loose and was now attached only by one frozen sleeve, they again came within sound of the weird moan of the willows, and again emerged on the open fields. The storm, far from ceasing, seemed to have grown yet stronger. The road was completely covered with drifting snow, and only the stakes showed that they had not lost their way. But even the stakes ahead of them were not easy to see, since the wind blew in their faces.

Vasíli Andréevich screwed up his eyes, bent down his head, and looked out for the way-marks, but trusted mainly to the horse's sagacity, letting it take its own way. And the horse really did not lose the road but followed its windings, turning now to the right and now to the left and sensing it under his feet, so that though the snow fell thicker and the wind strengthened they still continued to see way-marks now to the left and now to the right of them.

182

So they travelled on for about ten minutes, when suddenly, through the slanting screen of wind-driven snow, something black showed up which moved in front of the horse.

This was another sledge with fellow-travellers. Mukhórty overtook them, and struck his hoofs against the back of the sledge in front of him.

"Pass on . . . hey there . . . get in front!" cried voices from the sledge.

Vasíli Andréevich swerved aside to pass the other sledge. In it sat three men and a woman, evidently visitors returning from a feast. One peasant was whacking the snow-covered croup of their little horse with a long switch, and the other two sitting in front waved their arms and shouted something. The woman, completely wrapped up and covered with snow, sat drowsing and bumping at the back.

"Who are you?" shouted Vasíli Andréevich.

"From A-a-a . . ." was all that could be heard.

"I say, where are you from?"

"From A-a-a-a!" one of the peasants shouted with all his might, but still it was impossible to make out who they were.

"Get along! Keep up!" shouted another, ceaselessly beating his horse with the switch.

"So you're from a feast, it seems?"

"Go on, go on! Faster, Simon! Get in front! Faster!"

The wings of the sledges bumped against one another, almost got jammed but managed to separate, and the peasants' sledge began to fall behind.

Their shaggy, big-bellied horse, all covered with snow, breathed heavily under the low shaft-bow and, evidently using the last of its strength, vainly endeavored to escape from the switch, hobbling with its short legs through the deep snow which it threw up under itself.

Its muzzle, young-looking, with the nether lip drawn up like

183

that of a fish, nostrils distended and ears pressed back from fear, kept up for a few seconds near Nikíta's shoulder and then began to fall behind.

"Just see what liquor does!" said Nikíta. "They've tired that little horse to death. What pagans!"

For a few minutes they heard the panting of the tired little horse and the drunken shouting of the peasants. Then the panting and the shouts died away, and around them nothing could be heard but the whistling of the wind in their ears and now and then the squeak of their sledge-runners over a wind-swept part of the road.

This encounter cheered and enlivened Vasíli Andréevich, and he drove on more boldly without examining the way-marks, urging on the horse and trusting to him.

Nikíta had nothing to do, and as usual in such circumstances he drowsed, making up for much sleepless time. Suddenly the horse stopped and Nikíta nearly fell forward onto his nose.

"You know we're off the track again!" said Vasíli Andréevich.

"How's that?"

"Why, there are no way-marks to be seen. We must have got off the road again."

"Well, if we've lost the road we must find it," said Nikíta curtly, and getting out and stepping lightly on his pigeon-toed feet he started once more going about on the snow.

He walked about for a long time, now disappearing and now reappearing, and finally he came back.

"There is no road here. There may be farther on," he said, getting into the sledge.

It was already growing dark. The snow-storm had not increased but had also not subsided.

"If we could only hear those peasants!" said Vasíli Andréevich.

184

"Well, they haven't caught us up. We must have gone far astray. Or maybe they have lost their way too."

"Where are we to go then?" asked Vasíli Andréevich.

"Why, we must let the horse take its own way," said Nikíta. "He will take us right. Let me have the reins."

Vasíli Andréevich gave him the reins, the more willingly because his hands were beginning to feel frozen in his thick gloves.

Nikíta took the reins, but only held them, trying not to shake them and rejoicing at his favorite's sagacity. And indeed the clever horse, turning first one ear and then the other now to one side and then to the other, began to wheel round.

"The one thing he can't do is to talk," Nikíta kept saying. "See what he is doing! Go on, go on! You know best. That's it, that's it!"

The wind was now blowing from behind and it felt warmer.

"Yes, he's clever," Nikíta continued, admiring the horse. "A Kirgiz horse is strong but stupid. But this one—just see what he's doing with his ears! He doesn't need any telegraph. He can scent a mile off."

Before another half-hour had passed they saw something dark ahead of them—a wood or a village—and stakes again appeared to the right. They had evidently come out onto the road.

"Why, that's Grískino again!" Nikíta suddenly exclaimed.

And indeed, there on their left was that same barn with the snow flying from it, and farther on the same line with the frozen washing, shirts and trousers, which still fluttered desperately in the wind.

Again they drove into the street and again it grew quiet, warm, and cheerful, and again they could see the manure-stained street and hear voices and songs and the barking of a

185

dog. It was already so dark that there were lights in some of the windows.

Half-way through the village Vasíli Andréevich turned the horse towards a large double-fronted brick house and stopped at the porch.

Nikíta went to the lighted snow-covered window, in the rays of which flying snow-flakes glittered, and knocked at it with his whip.

"Who is there?" a voice replied to his knock.

"From Krestý, the Brekhunóvs, dear fellow," answered Nikíta. "Just come out for a minute."

Someone moved from the window, and a minute or two later there was the sound of the passage door as it came unstuck, then the latch of the outside door clicked and a tall white-bearded peasant, with a sheepskin coat thrown over his white holiday shirt, pushed his way out holding the door firmly against the wind, followed by a lad in a red shirt and high leather boots.

"Is that you, Andréevich?" asked the old man.

"Yes, friend, we've gone astray," said Vasíli Andréevich. "We wanted to get to Goryáchkin but found ourselves here. We went a second time but lost our way again."

"Just see how you have gone astray!" said the old man. "Petrúshka, go and open the gate!" he added, turning to the lad in the red shirt.

"All right," said the lad in a cheerful voice, and ran back into the passage.

"But we're not staying the night," said Vasíli Andréevich.

"Where will you go in the night? You'd better stay!"

"I'd be glad to, but I must go on. It's business, and it can't be helped."

"Well, warm yourself at least. The samovár is just ready."

"Warm myself? Yes, I'll do that," said Vasíli Andréevich.

186

"It won't get darker. The moon will rise and it will be lighter. Let's go in and warm ourselves, Nikíta."

"Well, why not? Let us warm ourselves," replied Nikíta, who was stiff with cold and anxious to warm his frozen limbs.

Vasíli Andréevich went into the room with the old man, and Nikíta drove through the gate opened for him by Petrúshka, by whose advice he backed the horse under the shed. The ground was covered with manure and the tall bow over the horse's head caught against the beam. The hens and the cock had already settled to roost there, and clucked peevishly, clinging to the beam with their claws. The disturbed sheep shied and rushed aside trampling the frozen manure with their hooves. The dog yelped desperately with fright and anger and then burst out barking like a puppy at the stranger.

Nikíta talked to them all, excused himself to the fowls and assured them that he would not disturb them again, rebuked the sheep for being frightened without knowing why, and kept soothing the dog, while he tied up the horse.

"Now that will be all right," he said, knocking the snow off his clothes. "Just hear how he barks!" he added, turning to the dog. "Be quiet, stupid! Be quiet. You are only troubling yourself for nothing. We're not thieves, we're friends. . . ."

"And these are, it's said, the three domestic counsellors," remarked the lad, and with his strong arms he pushed under the shed the sledge that had remained outside.

"Why counsellors?" asked Nikíta.

"That's what is printed in Paulson. A thief creeps to a house —the dog barks, that means, 'Be on your guard!' The cock crows, that means, 'Get up!' The cat licks herself—that means, 'A welcome guest is coming. Get ready to receive him!' " said the lad with a smile.

Petrúshka could read and write and knew Paulson's primer, his only book, almost by heart, and he was fond of quoting

187

sayings from it that he thought suited the occasion, especially when he had had something to drink, as to-day.

"That's so," said Nikíta.

"You must be chilled through and through," said Petrúshka.

"Yes, I am rather," said Nikíta, and they went across the yard and the passage into the house.

IV

The household to which Vasíli Andréevich had come was one of the richest in the village. The family had five allotments, besides renting other land. They had six horses, three cows, two calves, and some twenty sheep. There were twenty-two members belonging to the homestead: four married sons, six grandchildren (one of whom, Petrúshka, was married), two greatgrandchildren, three orphans, and four daughters-in-law with their babies. It was one of the few homesteads that remained still undivided, but even here the dull internal work of disintegration which would inevitably lead to separation had already begun, starting as usual among the women. Two sons were living in Moscow as water-carriers, and one was in the army. At home now were the old man and his wife, their second son who managed the homestead, the eldest who had come from Moscow for the holiday, and all the women and children. Besides these members of the family there was a visitor, a neighbor who was godfather to one of the children.

Over the table in the room hung a lamp with a shade, which brightly lit up the tea-things, a bottle of vódka, and some refreshments, besides illuminating the brick walls, which in the far corner were hung with icons on both sides of which were pictures. At the head of the table sat Vasíli Andréevich in a black sheepskin coat, sucking his frozen moustache and observ-

188

ing the room and the people around him with his prominent hawk-like eyes. With him sat the old, bald, white-bearded master of the house in a white homespun shirt, and next him the son home from Moscow for the holiday—a man with a sturdy back and powerful shoulders and clad in a thin print shirt—then the second son, also broad-shouldered, who acted as head of the house, and then a lean red-haired peasant—the neighbor.

Having had a drink of vódka and something to eat, they were about to take tea, and the samovár standing on the floor beside the brick oven was already humming. The children could be seen in the top bunks and on the top of the oven. A woman sat on a lower bunk with a cradle beside her. The old housewife, her face covered with wrinkles which creased even her lips, was waiting on Vasíli Andréevich.

As Nikíta entered the house she was offering her guest a small tumbler of thick glass which she had just filled with vódka.

"Don't refuse, Vasíli Andréevich, you mustn't! Wish us a merry feast. Drink it, dear!" she said.

The sight and smell of vódka, especially now when he was chilled through and tired out, much disturbed Nikíta's mind. He frowned, and having shaken the snow off his cap and coat, stopped in front of the icons as if not seeing anyone, crossed himself three times, and bowed to the icons. Then, turning to the old master of the house and bowing first to him, then to all those at table, then to the women who stood by the oven, and muttering: "A merry holiday!" he began taking off his outer things without looking at the table.

"Why, you're all covered with hoar-frost, old fellow!" said the eldest brother, looking at Nikíta's snow-covered face, eyes, and beard.

Nikíta took off his coat, shook it again, hung it up beside the oven, and came up to the table. He too was offered vódka. He

189

went through a moment of painful hesitation and nearly took up the glass and emptied the clear fragrant liquid down his throat, but he glanced at Vasíli Andréevich, remembered his oath and the boots that he had sold for drink, recalled the cooper, remembered his son for whom he had promised to buy a horse by spring, sighed, and declined it.

"I don't drink, thank you kindly," he said frowning, and sat down on a bench near the second window.

"How's that?" asked the eldest brother.

"I just don't drink," replied Nikíta without lifting his eyes but looking askance at his scanty beard and moustache and getting the icicles out of them.

"It's not good for him," said Vasíli Andréevich, munching a cracknel after emptying his glass.

"Well, then, have some tea," said the kindly old hostess. "You must be chilled through, good soul. Why are you women dawdling so with the samovár?"

"It is ready," said one of the young women, and after flicking with her apron the top of the samovár which was now boiling over, she carried it with an effort to the table, raised it, and set it down with a thud.

Meanwhile Vasíli Andréevich was telling how he had lost his way, how they had come back twice to this same village, and how they had gone astray and had met some drunken peasants. Their hosts were surprised, explained where and why they had missed their way, said who the tipsy people they had met were, and told them how they ought to go.

"A little child could find the way to Molchánovka from here. All you have to do is to take the right turning from the high road. There's a bush you can see just there. But you didn't even get that far!" said the neighbor.

"You'd better stay the night. The women will make up beds for you," said the old woman persuasively.

190

"You could go on in the morning and it would be pleasanter," said the old man, confirming what his wife had said.

"I can't, friend. Business!" said Vasíli Andréevich. "Lose an hour and you can't catch it up in a year," he added, remembering the grove and the dealers who might snatch that deal from him. "We shall get there, shan't we?" he said, turning to Nikíta.

Nikíta did not answer for some time, apparently still intent on thawing out his beard and moustache.

"If only we don't go astray again," he replied gloomily.

He was gloomy because he passionately longed for some vódka, and the only thing that could assuage that longing was tea and he had not yet been offered any.

"But we have only to reach the turning and then we shan't go wrong. The road will be through the forest the whole way," said Vasíli Andréevich.

"It's just as you please, Vasíli Andréevich. If we're to go, let us go," said Nikíta, taking the glass of tea he was offered.

"We'll drink our tea and be off."

Nikíta said nothing but only shook his head, and carefully pouring some tea into his saucer began warming his hands, the fingers of which were always swollen with hard work, over the steam. Then, biting off a tiny bit of sugar, he bowed to his hosts, said, "Your health!" and drew in the steaming liquid.

"If somebody would see us as far as the turning," said Vasíli Andréevich.

"Well, we can do that," said the eldest son. "Petrúshka will harness and go that far with you."

"Well, then, put in the horse, lad, and I shall be thankful to you for it."

"Oh, what for, dear man?" said the kindly old woman. "We are heartily glad to do it."

"Petrúshka, go and put in the mare," said the eldest brother.

191

"All right," replied Petrúshka with a smile, and promptly snatching his cap down from a nail he ran away to harness.

While the horse was being harnessed the talk returned to the point at which it had stopped when Vasíli Andréevich drove up to the window. The old man had been complaining to his neighbor, the village elder, about his third son who had not sent him anything for the holiday though he had sent a French shawl to his wife.

"The young people are getting out of hand," said the old man.

"And how they do!" said the neighbor. "There's no managing them! They know too much. There's Demóchkin now, who broke his father's arm. It's all from being too clever, it seems."

Nikíta listened, watched their faces, and evidently would have liked to share in the conversation, but he was too busy drinking his tea and only nodded his head approvingly. He emptied one tumbler after another and grew warmer and warmer and more and more comfortable. The talk continued on the same subject for a long time—the harmfulness of a household dividing up—and it was clearly not an abstract discussion but concerned the question of a separation in that house; a separation demanded by the second son who sat there morosely silent.

It was evidently a sore subject and absorbed them all, but out of propriety they did not discuss their private affairs before strangers. At last, however, the old man could not restrain himself, and with tears in his eyes declared that he would not consent to a break-up of the family during his lifetime, that his house was prospering, thank God, but that if they separated they would all have to go begging.

"Just like the Matvéevs," said the neighbor. "They used to have a proper house, but now they've split up none of them has anything."

192

"And that is what you want to happen to us," said the old man, turning to his son.

The son made no reply and there was an awkward pause. The silence was broken by Petrúshka, who having harnessed the horse had returned to the hut a few minutes before this and had been listening all the time with a smile.

"There's a fable about that in Paulson," he said. "A father gave his sons a broom to break. At first they could not break it, but when they took it twig by twig they broke it easily. And it's the same here," and he gave a broad smile. "I'm ready!" he added.

"If you're ready, let's go," said Vasíli Andréevich. "And as to separating, don't you allow it, grandfather. You got everything together and you're the master. Go to the Justice of the Peace. He'll say how things should be done."

"He carries on so, carries on so," the old man continued in a whining tone. "There's no doing anything with him. It's as if the devil possessed him."

Nikíta having meanwhile finished his fifth tumbler of tea laid it on its side instead of turning it upside down, hoping to be offered a sixth glass. But there was no more water in the samovár, so the hostess did not fill it up for him. Besides, Vasíli Andréevich was putting his things on, so there was nothing for it but for Nikíta to get up too, put back into the sugar-basin the lump of sugar he had nibbled all round, wipe his perspiring face with the skirt of his sheepskin, and go to put on his overcoat.

Having put it on he sighed deeply, thanked his hosts, said good-bye, and went out of the warm bright room into the cold dark passage, through which the wind was howling and where snow was blowing through the cracks of the shaking door, and from there into the yard.

Petrúshka stood in his sheepskin in the middle of the yard

193

by his horse, repeating some lines from Paulson's primer. He said with a smile:

> "Storms with mist the sky conceal,
> Snowy circles wheeling wild
> Now like savage beast 'twill howl,
> And now 'tis wailing like a child."

Nikíta nodded approvingly as he arranged the reins.

The old man, seeing Vasíli Andréevich off, brought a lantern into the passage to show him a light, but it was blown out at once. And even in the yard it was evident that the snow-storm had become more violent.

"Well, this is weather!" thought Vasíli Andréevich. "Perhaps we may not get there after all. But there is nothing to be done. Business! Besides, we have got ready, our host's horse has been harnessed, and we'll get there with God's help!"

Their aged host also thought they ought not to go, but he had already tried to persuade them to stay and had not been listened to.

"It's no use asking them again. Maybe my age makes me timid. They'll get there all right, and at least we shall get to bed in good time and without any fuss," he thought.

Petrúshka did not think of danger. He knew the road and the whole district so well, and the lines about "snowy circles wheeling wild" described what was happening outside so aptly that it cheered him up. Nikíta did not wish to go at all, but he had been accustomed not to have his own way and to serve others for so long that there was no one to hinder the departing travellers.

V

Vasíli Andréevich went over to his sledge, found it with difficulty in the darkness, climbed in and took the reins.

"Go on in front!" he cried.

Petrúshka kneeling in his low sledge started his horse. Muk-hórty, who had been neighing for some time past, now scenting a mare ahead of him started after her, and they drove out into the street. They drove again through the outskirts of the village and along the same road, past the yard where the frozen linen had hung (which, however, was no longer to be seen), past the same barn, which was now snowed up almost to the roof and from which the snow was still endlessly pouring, past the same dismally moaning, whistling, and swaying willows, and again entered into the sea of blustering snow raging from above and below. The wind was so strong that when it blew from the side and the travellers steered against it, it tilted the sledges and turned the horses to one side. Petrúshka drove his good mare in front at a brisk trot and kept shouting lustily. Mukhórty pressed after her.

After travelling so for about ten minutes, Petrúshka turned round and shouted something. Neither Vasíli Andréevich nor Nikíta could hear anything because of the wind, but they guessed that they had arrived at the turning. In fact Petrúshka had turned to the right, and now the wind that had blown from the side blew straight in their faces, and through the snow they saw something dark on their right. It was the bush at the turning.

"Well now, God speed you!"

"Thank you, Petrúshka!"

"Storms with mist the sky conceal!" shouted Petrúshka as he disappeared.

"There's a poet for you!" muttered Vasíli Andréevich, pull-ing at the reins.

"Yes, a fine lad—a true peasant," said Nikíta.

They drove on.

Nikíta, wrapping his coat closely about him and pressing his head down so close to his shoulders that his short beard covered his throat, sat silently, trying not to lose the warmth he had

195

obtained while drinking tea in the house. Before him he saw the straight lines of the shafts which constantly deceived him into thinking they were a well-travelled road, and the horse's swaying crupper with his knotted tail blown to one side, and farther ahead the high shaft-bow and the swaying head and neck of the horse with his waving mane. Now and then he caught sight of a way-sign, so that he knew they were still on a road and that there was nothing for him to be concerned about.

Vasíli Andréevich drove on, leaving it to the horse to keep to the road. But Mukhórty, though he had had a breathing-space in the village, ran reluctantly, and seemed now and then to get off the road, so that Vasíli Andréevich had repeatedly to correct him.

"Here's a stake to the right, and another, and here's a third," Vasíli Andréevich counted, "and here in front is the forest," thought he, as he looked at something dark in front of him. But what had seemed to him a forest was only a bush. They passed the bush and drove on for another hundred yards but there was no fourth way-mark nor any forest.

"We must reach the forest soon," thought Vasíli Andréevich, and animated by the vódka and the tea he did not stop but shook the reins, and the good obedient horse responded, now ambling, now slowly trotting in the direction in which he was sent, though he knew that he was not going the right way. Ten minutes went by, but there was still no forest.

"There now, we must be astray again," said Vasíli Andréevich, pulling up.

Nikíta silently got out of the sledge and holding his coat, which the wind now wrapped closely about him and now almost tore off, started to feel about in the snow, going first to one side and then to the other. Three or four times he was completely lost to sight. At last he returned and took the reins from Vasíli Andréevich's hand.

196

"We must go to the right," he said sternly and peremptorily, as he turned the horse.

"Well, if it's to the right, go to the right," said Vasíli Andréevich, yielding up the reins to Nikíta and thrusting his freezing hands into his sleeves.

Nikíta did not reply.

"Now then, friend, stir yourself!" he shouted to the horse, but in spite of the shake of the reins Mukhórty moved only at a walk.

The snow in places was up to his knees, and the sledge moved by fits and starts with his every movement.

Nikíta took the whip that hung over the front of the sledge and struck him once. The good horse, unused to the whip, sprang forward and moved at a trot, but immediately fell back into an amble and then to a walk. So they went on for five minutes. It was dark and the snow whirled from above and rose from below, so that sometimes the shaft-bow could not be seen. At times the sledge seemed to stand still and the field to run backwards. Suddenly the horse stopped abruptly, evidently aware of something close in front of him. Nikíta again sprang lightly out, throwing down the reins, and went ahead to see what had brought him to a standstill, but hardly had he made a step in front of the horse before his feet slipped and he went rolling down an incline.

"Whoa, whoa, whoa!" he said to himself as he fell, and he tried to stop his fall but could not, and only stopped when his feet plunged into a thick layer of snow that had drifted to the bottom of the hollow.

The fringe of a drift of snow that hung on the edge of the hollow, disturbed by Nikíta's fall, showered down on him and got inside his collar.

"What a thing to do!" said Nikíta reproachfully, addressing

197

the drift and the hollow and shaking the snow from under his collar.

"Nikíta! Hey, Nikíta!" shouted Vasíli Andréevich from above.

But Nikíta did not reply. He was too occupied in shaking out the snow and searching for the whip he had dropped when rolling down the incline. Having found the whip he tried to climb straight up the bank where he had rolled down, but it was impossible to do so: he kept rolling down again, and so he had to go along at the foot of the hollow to find a way up. About seven yards farther on he managed with difficulty to crawl up the incline on all fours, then he followed the edge of the hollow back to the place where the horse should have been. He could not see either horse or sledge, but as he walked against the wind he heard Vasíli Andréevich's shouts and Mukhórty's neighing, calling him.

"I'm coming! I'm coming! What are you cackling for?" he muttered.

Only when he had come up to the sledge could he make out the horse, and Vasíli Andréevich standing beside it and looking gigantic.

"Where the devil did you vanish to? We must go back, if only to Gríshkino," he began reproaching Nikíta.

"I'd be glad to get back, Vasíli Andréevich, but which way are we to go? There is such a ravine here that if we once get in it we shan't get out again. I got stuck so fast there myself that I could hardly get out."

"What shall we do, then? We can't stay here! We must go somewhere!" said Vasíli Andréevich.

Nikíta said nothing. He seated himself in the sledge with his back to the wind, took off his boots, shook out the snow that had got into them, and taking some straw from the bottom of the sledge, carefully plugged with it a hole in his left boot.

198

Vasíli Andréevich remained silent, as though now leaving everything to Nikíta. Having put his boots on again, Nikíta drew his feet into the sledge, put on his mittens and took up the reins, and directed the horse along the side of the ravine. But they had not gone a hundred yards before the horse again stopped short. The ravine was in front of him again.

Nikíta again climbed out and again trudged about in the snow. He did this for a considerable time and at last appeared on the side opposite to that from which he had started.

"Vasíli Andréevich, are you alive?" he called out.

"Here!" replied Vasíli Andréevich. "Well, what now?"

"I can't make anything out. It's too dark. There's nothing but ravines. We must drive against the wind again."

They set off once more. Again Nikíta went stumbling through the snow, again he fell in, again climbed out and trudged about, and at last quite out of breath he sat down beside the sledge.

"Well, how now?" asked Vasíli Andréevich.

"Why, I am quite worn out and the horse won't go."

"Then what's to be done?"

"Why, wait a minute."

Nikíta went away again but soon returned.

"Follow me!" he said, going in front of the horse.

Vasíli Andréevich no longer gave orders but implicitly did what Nikíta told him.

"Here, follow me!" Nikíta shouted, stepping quickly to the right, and seizing the rein he led Mukhórty down towards a snow-drift.

At first the horse held back, then he jerked forward, hoping to leap the drift, but he had not the strength and sank into it up to his collar.

"Get out!" Nikíta called to Vasíli Andréevich who still sat in the sledge, and taking hold of one shaft he moved the sledge

199

closer to the horse. "It's hard, brother!" he said to Mukhórty, "but it can't be helped. Make an effort! Now, now, just a little one!" he shouted.

The horse gave a tug, then another, but failed to clear himself and settled down again as if considering something.

"Now, brother, this won't do!" Nikíta admonished him. "Now once more!"

Again Nikíta tugged at the shaft on his side, and Vasíli Andréevich did the same on the other.

Mukhórty lifted his head and then gave a sudden jerk.

"That's it! That's it!" cried Nikíta. "Don't be afraid—you won't sink!"

One plunge, another, and a third, and at last Mukhórty was out of the snow-drift, and stood still, breathing heavily and shaking the snow off himself. Nikíta wished to lead him farther, but Vasíli Andréevich, in his two fur coats, was so out of breath that he could not walk farther and dropped into the sledge.

"Let me get my breath!" he said, unfastening the kerchief with which he had tied the collar of his fur coat at the village.

"It's all right here. You lie there," said Nikíta. "I will lead him along." And with Vasíli Andréevich in the sledge he led the horse by the bridle about ten paces down and then up a slight rise, and stopped.

The place where Nikíta had stopped was not completely in the hollow where the snow sweeping down from the hillocks might have buried them altogether, but still it was partly sheltered from the wind by the side of the ravine. There were moments when the wind seemed to abate a little, but that did not last long and as if to make up for that respite the storm swept down with tenfold vigor and tore and whirled the more fiercely. Such a gust struck them at the moment when Vasíli Andréevich, having recovered his breath, got out of the sledge and went up to Nikíta to consult him as to what they should do. They both

200

bent down involuntarily and waited till the violence of the squall should have passed. Mukhórty too laid back his ears and shook his head discontentedly. As soon as the violence of the blast had abated a little, Nikíta took off his mittens, stuck them into his belt, breathed on to his hands, and began to undo the straps of the shaft-bow.

"What's that you are doing there?" asked Vasíli Andréevich.

"Unharnessing. What else is there to do? I have no strength left," said Nikíta as though excusing himself.

"Can't we drive somewhere?"

"No, we can't. We shall only kill the horse. Why, the poor beast is not himself now," said Nikíta, pointing to the horse, which was standing submissively waiting for what might come, with his steep wet sides heaving heavily. "We shall have to stay the night here," he said, as if preparing to spend the night at an inn, and he proceeded to unfasten the collar-straps. The buckles came undone.

"But shan't we be frozen?" remarked Vasíli Andréevich.

"Well, if we are we can't help it," said Nikíta.

VI

Although Vasíli Andréevich felt quite warm in his two fur coats, especially after struggling in the snow-drift, a cold shiver ran down his back on realizing that he must really spend the night where they were. To calm himself he sat down in the sledge and got out his cigarettes and matches.

Nikíta meanwhile unharnessed Mukhórty. He unstrapped the belly-band and the back-band, took away the reins and removed the shaft-bow, talking to him all the time to encourage him.

"Now come out! Come out!" he said, leading him clear of the shafts. "Now we'll tie you up here and I'll put down some straw

201

and take off your bridle. When you've had a bite you'll feel more cheerful."

But Mukhórty was restless and evidently not comforted by Nikíta's remarks. He stepped now on one foot and now on another, and pressed close against the sledge, turning his back to the wind and rubbing his head on Nikíta's sleeve. Then, as if not to pain Nikíta by refusing his offer of the straw he put before him, he hurriedly snatched a wisp out of the sledge, but immediately decided that it was now no time to think of straw and threw it down, and the wind instantly scattered it, carried it away, and covered it with snow.

"Now we will set up a signal," said Nikíta, and turning the front of the sledge to the wind he tied the shafts together with a strap and set them up on end in front of the sledge. "There now, when the snow covers us up, good folk will see the shafts and dig us out," he said, slapping his mittens together and putting them on. "That's what the old folk taught us!"

Vasíli Andréevich meanwhile had unfastened his coat, and holding its skirts up for shelter, struck one sulphur match after another on the steel box. But his hands trembled, and one match after another either did not kindle or was blown out by the wind just as he was lifting it to the cigarette. At last a match did burn up, and its flame lit up for a moment the fur of his coat, his hand with the gold ring on the bent forefinger, and the snow-sprinkled oat-straw that stuck out from under the drugget. The cigarette lighted, he eagerly took a whiff or two, inhaled the smoke, let it out through his moustache, and would have inhaled again, but the wind tore off the burning tobacco and whirled it away as it had done the straw.

But even these few puffs had cheered him.

"If we must spend the night here, we must!" he said with decision. "Wait a bit, I'll arrange a flag as well," he added, picking up the kerchief which he had thrown down in the sledge after taking it from round his collar, and drawing off his gloves and standing up on the front of the sledge and stretching himself to reach the strap, he tied the kerchief to it with a tight knot.

The kerchief immediately began to flutter wildly, now clinging round the shaft, now suddenly streaming out, stretching and flapping.

"Just see what a fine flag!" said Vasíli Andréevich, admiring his handiwork and letting himself down into the sledge. "We should be warmer together, but there's not room enough for two," he added.

"I'll find a place," said Nikíta. "But I must cover up the horse first—he sweated so, poor thing. Let go!" he added, drawing the drugget from under Vasíli Andréevich.

Having got the drugget he folded it in two, and after taking off the breechband and pad, covered Mukhórty with it.

"Anyhow it will be warmer, silly!" he said, putting back the breechband and the pad on the horse over the drugget. Then having finished that business he returned to the sledge, and addressing Vasíli Andréevich, said: "You won't need the sackcloth, will you? And let me have some straw."

And having taken these things from under Vasíli Andréevich, Nikíta went behind the sledge, dug out a hole for himself in the snow, put straw into it, wrapped his coat well round him, covered himself with the sackcloth, and pulling his cap well down seated himself on the straw he had spread, and leant against the wooden back of the sledge to shelter himself from the wind and the snow.

Vasíli Andréevich shook his head disapprovingly at what Nikíta was doing, as in general he disapproved of the peasants' stupidity and lack of education, and he began to settle himself down for the night.

He smoothed the remaining straw over the bottom of the sledge, putting more of it under his side, then he thrust his

203

hands into his sleeves and settled down, sheltering his head in the corner of the sledge from the wind in front.

He did not wish to sleep. He lay and thought: thought ever of the one thing that constituted the sole aim, meaning, pleasure, and pride of his life—of how much money he had made and might still make, of how much other people he knew had made and possessed, and of how those others had made and were making it, and how he, like them, might still make much more. The purchase of the Goryáchkin grove was a matter of immense importance to him. By that one deal he hoped to make perhaps ten thousand rúbles. He began mentally to reckon the value of the wood he had inspected in autumn, and on five acres of which he had counted all the trees.

"The oaks will go for sledge-runners. The undergrowth will take care of itself, and there'll still be some thirty sázheens of fire-wood left on each desyatín," said he to himself. "That means there will be at least two hundred and twenty-five rúbles' worth left on each desyatín. Fifty-six desyatíns mean fifty-six hundreds, and fifty-six hundreds, and fifty-six tens, and another fifty-six tens, and then fifty-six fives. . . ." He saw that it came out to more than twelve thousand rúbles, but could not reckon it up exactly without a counting-frame. "But I won't give ten thousand, anyhow. I'll give about eight thousand with a deduction on account of the glades. I'll grease the surveyor's palm— give him a hundred rúbles, or a hundred and fifty, and he'll reckon that there are some five desyatíns of glade to be deducted. And he'll let it go for eight thousand. Three thousand cash down. That'll move him, no fear!" he thought, and he pressed his pocket-book with his forearm.

"God only knows how we missed the turning. The forest ought to be there, and a watchman's hut, and dogs barking. But the damned things don't bark when they're wanted." He turned his collar down from his ear and listened, but as before only the whistling of the wind could be heard, the flapping and fluttering of the kerchief tied to the shafts, and the pelting of the snow against the woodwork of the sledge. He again covered up his ear.

"If I had known I would have stayed the night. Well, no matter, we'll get there to-morrow. It's only one day lost. And the others won't travel in such weather." Then he remembered that on the 9th he had to receive payment from the butcher for his oxen. "He meant to come himself, but he won't find me, and my wife won't know how to receive the money. She doesn't know the right way of doing things," he thought, recalling how at their party the day before she had not known how to treat the police-officer who was their guest. "Of course she's only a woman! Where could she have seen anything? In my father's time what was our house like? Just a rich peasant's house: just an oat-mill and an inn—that was the whole property. But what have I done in these fifteen years? A shop, two taverns, a flour-mill, a grain-store, two farms leased out, and a house with an iron-roofed barn," he thought proudly. "Not as it was in father's time! Who is talked of in the whole district now? Brekhunóv! And why? Because I stick to business. I take trouble, not like others who lie abed or waste their time on foolishness while I don't sleep of nights. Blizzard or no blizzard I start out. So business gets done. They think money-making is a joke. No, take pains and rack your brain! You get overtaken out of doors at night, like this, or keep awake night after night till the thoughts whirling in your head make the pillow turn," he meditated with pride. "They think people get on through luck. After all, the Mirónovs are now millionaires. And why? Take pains and God gives. If only He grants me health!"

The thought that he might himself be a millionaire like Mirónov, who began with nothing, so excited Vasíli Andréevich that he felt the need of talking to somebody. But there was

205

no one to talk to. . . . If only he could have reached Goryách-kin he would have talked to the landlord and shown him a thing or two.

"Just see how it blows! It will snow up so deep that we shan't be able to get out in the morning!" he thought, listening to a gust of wind that blew against the front of the sledge, bending it and lashing the snow against it. He raised himself and looked round. All he could see through the whirling darkness was Mukhórty's dark head, his back covered by the fluttering drugget, and his thick knotted tail; while all round, in front and behind, was the same fluctuating whity darkness, sometimes seeming to get a little lighter and sometimes growing denser still.

"A pity I listened to Nikíta," he thought. "We ought to have driven on. We should have come out somewhere, if only back to Grishkino and stayed the night at Tarás's. As it is we must sit here all night. But what was I thinking about? Yes, that God gives to those who take trouble, but not to loafers, lie-abeds, or fools. I must have a smoke!"

He sat down again, got out his cigarette-case, and stretched himself flat on his stomach, screening the matches with the skirt of his coat. But the wind found its way in and put out match after match. At last he got one to burn and lit a cigarette. He was very glad that he had managed to do what he wanted, and though the wind smoked more of the cigarette than he did, he still got two or three puffs and felt more cheerful. He again leant back, wrapped himself up, started reflecting and remembering, and suddenly and quite unexpectedly lost consciousness and fell asleep.

Suddenly something seemed to give him a push and awoke him. Whether it was Mukhórty who had pulled some straw from under him, or whether something within him had startled him, at all events it woke him, and his heart began to beat faster and

206

faster so that the sledge seemed to tremble under him. He opened his eyes. Everything around him was just as before. "It looks lighter," he thought. "I expect it won't be long before dawn." But he at once remembered that it was lighter because the moon had risen. He sat up and looked first at the horse. Mukhórty still stood with his back to the wind, shivering all over. One side of the drugget, which was completely covered with snow, had been blown back, the breeching had slipped down and the snow-covered head with its waving forelock and mane were now more visible. Vasíli Andréevich leant over the back of the sledge and looked behind. Nikíta still sat in the same position in which he had settled himself. The sacking with which he was covered, and his legs, were thickly covered with snow.

"If only that peasant doesn't freeze to death! His clothes are so wretched. I may be held responsible for him. What shiftless people they are—such a want of education," thought Vasíli Andréevich, and he felt like taking the drugget off the horse and putting it over Nikíta, but it would be very cold to get out and move about and, moreover, the horse might freeze to death. "Why did I bring him with me? It was all her stupidity!" he thought, recalling his unloved wife, and he rolled over into his old place at the front part of the sledge. "My uncle once spent a whole night like this," he reflected, "and was all right." But another case came at once to his mind. "But when they dug Sebastian out he was dead—stiff like a frozen carcass. If I'd only stopped the night in Gríshkino all this would not have happened!"

And wrapping his coat carefully round him so that none of the warmth of the fur should be wasted but should warm him all over, neck, knees, and feet, he shut his eyes and tried to sleep again. But try as he would he could not get drowsy, on the contrary he felt wide awake and animated. Again he began counting his gains and the debts due to him, again he began bragging to himself and feeling pleased with himself and his position, but all this was continually disturbed by a stealthily approaching fear and by the unpleasant regret that he had not remained in Gríshkino.

"How different it would be to be lying warm on a bench!" He turned over several times in his attempts to get into a more comfortable position better sheltered from the wind, he wrapped up his legs closer, shut his eyes, and lay still. But either his legs in their strong felt boots began to ache from being bent in one position, or the wind blew in somewhere, and after lying still for a short time he again began to recall the disturbing fact that he might now have been lying quietly in the warm hut at Gríshkino. He again sat up, turned about, muffled himself up, and settled down once more.

Once he fancied that he heard a distant cock-crow. He felt glad, turned down his coat-collar and listened with strained attention, but in spite of all his efforts nothing could be heard but the wind whistling between the shafts, the flapping of the kerchief, and the snow pelting against the frame of the sledge.

Nikíta sat just as he had done all the time, not moving and not even answering Vasíli Andréevich who had addressed him a couple of times. "He doesn't care a bit—he's probably asleep!" thought Vasíli Andréevich with vexation, looking behind the sledge at Nikíta who was covered with a thick layer of snow.

Vasíli Andréevich got up and lay down again some twenty times. It seemed to him that the night would never end. "It must be getting near morning," he thought, getting up and looking around. "Let's have a look at my watch. It will be cold to unbutton, but if I only know that it's getting near morning I shall at any rate feel more cheerful. We could begin harnessing."

In the depth of his heart Vasíli Andréevich knew that it could not yet be near morning, but he was growing more and more afraid, and wished both to get to know and yet to deceive himself. He carefully undid the fastening of his sheepskin, pushed in his hand, and felt about for a long time before he got to his waistcoat. With great difficulty he managed to draw out his silver watch with its enamelled flower design, and tried to make out the time. He could not see anything without a light. Again he went down on his knees and elbows as he had done when he lighted a cigarette, got out his matches, and proceeded to strike one. This time he went to work more carefully, and feeling with his fingers for a match with the largest head and the greatest amount of phosphorus, lit it at the first try. Bringing the face of the watch under the light he could hardly believe his eyes. . . . It was only ten minutes past twelve. Almost the whole night was still before him.

"Oh, how long the night is!" he thought, feeling a cold shudder run down his back, and having fastened his fur coats again and wrapped himself up, he snuggled into a corner of the sledge intending to wait patiently. Suddenly, above the monotonous roar of the wind, he clearly distinguished another new and living sound. It steadily strengthened, and having become quite clear diminished just as gradually. Beyond all doubt it was a wolf, and he was so near that the movement of his jaws as he changed his cry was brought down the wind. Vasíli Andréevich turned back the collar of his coat and listened attentively. Mukhórty too strained to listen, moving his ears, and when the wolf had ceased its howling he shifted from foot to foot and gave a warning snort. After this Vasíli Andréevich could not fall asleep again or even calm himself. The more he tried to think of his accounts, his business, his reputation, his worth and his wealth, the more and more was he mastered by fear; and regrets that he had not stayed the night at Gríshkino dominated and mingled in all his thoughts.

"Devil take the forest! Things were all right without it, thank God. Ah, if we had only put up for the night!" he said to himself. "They say it's drunkards that freeze," he thought, "and I have had some drink." And observing his sensations he noticed that he was beginning to shiver, without knowing whether it was from cold or from fear. He tried to wrap himself up and lie down as before, but could no longer do so. He could not stay in one position. He wanted to get up, to do something to master the gathering fear that was rising in him and against which he felt himself powerless. He again got out his cigarettes and matches, but only three matches were left and they were bad ones. The phosphorus rubbed off them all without lighting.

"The devil take you! Damned thing! Curse you!" he muttered, not knowing whom or what he was cursing, and he flung away the crushed cigarette. He was about to throw away the matchbox too, but checked the movement of his hand and put the box in his pocket instead. He was seized with such unrest that he could no longer remain in one spot. He climbed out of the sledge and standing with his back to the wind began to shift his belt again, fastening it lower down in the waist and tightening it.

"What's the use of lying and waiting for death? Better mount the horse and get away!" The thought suddenly occurred to him. "The horse will move when he has someone on his back. As for him," he thought of Nikíta—"it's all the same to him whether he lives or dies. What is his life worth? He won't grudge his life, but I have something to live for, thank God."

He untied the horse, threw the reins over his neck and tried to mount, but his coats and boots were so heavy that he failed. Then he clambered up in the sledge and tried to mount from there, but the sledge tilted under his weight, and he failed again. At last he drew Mukhórty nearer to the sledge, cautiously balanced on one side of it, and managed to lie on his stomach across the horse's back. After lying like that for a while he shifted forward once and again, threw a leg over, and finally

210

seated himself, supporting his feet on the loose breeching-straps. The shaking of the sledge awoke Nikíta. He raised himself, and it seemed to Vasíli Andréevich that he said something.

"Listen to such fools as you! Am I to die like this for nothing?" exclaimed Vasíli Andréevich. And tucking the loose skirts of his fur coat in under his knees, he turned the horse and rode away from the sledge in the direction in which he thought the forest and the forester's hut must be.

VII

From the time he had covered himself with the sackcloth and seated himself behind the sledge, Nikíta had not stirred. Like all those who live in touch with nature and have known want, he was patient and could wait for hours, even days, without growing restless or irritable. He heard his master call him, but did not answer because he did not want to move or talk. Though he still felt some warmth from the tea he had drunk and from his energetic struggle when clambering about in the snowdrift, he knew that this warmth would not last long and that he had no strength left to warm himself again by moving about, for he felt as tired as a horse when it stops and refuses to go further in spite of the whip, and its master sees that it must be fed before it can work again. The foot in the boot with a hole in it had already grown numb, and he could no longer feel his big toe. Besides that, his whole body began to feel colder and colder.

The thought that he might, and very probably would, die that night occurred to him, but did not seem particularly unpleasant or dreadful. It did not seem particularly unpleasant, because his whole life had been not a continual holiday, but on the contrary an unceasing round of toil of which he was beginning to feel weary. And it did not seem particularly dreadful, because besides the masters he had served here, like Vasíli Andréevich, he always felt himself dependent on the Chief Master, who had sent him into this life, and he knew that when dying he would still be in that Master's power and would not be ill-used by Him. "It seems a pity to give up what one is used to and accustomed to. But there's nothing to be done; I shall get used to the new things."

"Sins?" he thought, and remembered his drunkenness, the money that had gone on drink, how he had offended his wife, his cursing, his neglect of church and of the fasts, and all the things the priest blamed him for at confession. "Of course they are sins. But then, did I take them on of myself? That's evidently how God made me. Well, and the sins? Where am I to escape to?"

So at first he thought of what might happen to him that night, and then did not return to such thoughts but gave himself up to whatever recollections came into his head of themselves. Now he thought of Martha's arrival, of the drunkenness among the workers and his own renunciation of drink, then of their present journey and of Tarás's house and the talk about the breaking-up of the family, then of his own lad, and of Mukhórty now sheltered under the drugget, and then of his master who made the sledge creak as he tossed about in it. "I expect you're sorry yourself that you started out, dear man," he thought. "It would seem hard to leave a life such as his! It's not like the likes of us."

Then all these recollections began to grow confused and got mixed in his head, and he fell asleep.

But when Vasíli Andréevich, getting on the horse, jerked the sledge against the back of which Nikíta was leaning, and it shifted away and hit him in the back with one of its runners, he awoke and had to change his position whether he liked it or not. Straightening his legs with difficulty and shaking the snow off them he got up, and an agonizing cold immediately penetrated his whole body. On making out what was happening he called

212

to Vasíli Andréevich to leave him the drugget which the horse no longer needed, so that he might wrap himself in it.

But Vasíli Andréevich did not stop, but disappeared amid the powdery snow.

Left alone, Nikíta considered for a moment what he should do. He felt that he had not the strength to go off in search of a house. It was no longer possible to sit down in his old place— it was by now all filled with snow. He felt that he could not get warmer in the sledge either, for there was nothing to cover himself with, and his coat and sheepskin no longer warmed him at all. He felt as cold as though he had nothing on but a shirt. He became frightened. "Lord, heavenly Father!" he muttered, and was comforted by the consciousness that he was not alone but that there was One who heard him and would not abandon him. He gave a deep sigh, and keeping the sackcloth over his head he got inside the sledge and lay down in the place where his master had been.

But he could not get warm in the sledge either. At first he shivered all over, then the shivering ceased and little by little he began to lose consciousness. He did not know whether he was dying or falling asleep, but felt equally prepared for the one as for the other.

VIII

Meanwhile Vasíli Andréevich, with his feet and the ends of the reins, urged the horse on in the direction in which for some reason he expected the forest and the forester's hut to be. The snow covered his eyes and the wind seemed intent on stopping him, but bending forward and constantly lapping his coat over and pushing it between himself and the cold harness pad which prevented him from sitting properly, he kept urging the horse on. Mukhórty ambled on obediently though with difficulty, in the direction in which he was driven.

213

Vasíli Andréevich rode for about five minutes straight ahead, as he thought, seeing nothing but the horse's head and the white waste, and hearing only the whistle of the wind about the horse's ears and his coat-collar.

Suddenly a dark patch showed up in front of him. His heart beat with joy, and he rode towards the object, already seeing in imagination the walls of village houses. But the dark patch was not stationary, it kept moving; and it was not a village but some tall stalks of wormwood sticking up through the snow on the boundary between two fields, and desperately tossing about under the pressure of the wind which beat it all to one side and whistled through it. The sight of that wormwood tormented by the pitiless wind made Vasíli Andréevich shudder, he knew not why, and he hurriedly began urging the horse on, not noticing that when riding up to the wormwood he had quite changed his direction and was now heading the opposite way, though still imagining that he was riding towards where the hut should be. But the horse kept making towards the right, and Vasíli Andréevich kept guiding it to the left.

Again something dark appeared in front of him. Again he rejoiced, convinced that now it was certainly a village. But once more it was the same boundary line overgrown with wormwood, once more the same wormwood desperately tossed by the wind and carrying unreasoning terror to his heart. But its being the same wormwood was not all, for beside it there was a horse's track partly snowed over. Vasíli Andréevich stopped, stooped down and looked carefully. It was a horse-track only partially covered with snow, and could be none but his own horse's hoof-prints. He had evidently gone round in a small circle. "I shall perish like that!" he thought, and not to give way to his terror he urged on the horse still more, peering into the snowy darkness in which he saw only flitting and fitful points of light. Once he thought he heard the barking of dogs or the howling of wolves, but the sounds were so faint and indistinct that he did not know whether he heard them or merely imagined them, and he stopped and began to listen intently.

Suddenly some terrible, deafening cry resounded near his ears, and everything shivered and shook under him. He seized Mukhórty's neck, but that too was shaking all over and the terrible cry grew still more frightful. For some seconds Vasíli Andréevich could not collect himself or understand what was happening. It was only that Mukhórty, whether to encourage himself or to call for help, had neighed loudly and resonantly. "Ugh, you wretch! How you frightened me, damn you!" thought Vasíli Andréevich. But even when he understood the cause of his terror he could not shake it off.

"I must calm myself and think things over," he said to himself, but yet he could not stop, and continued to urge the horse on, without noticing that he was now going with the wind instead of against it. His body, especially between his legs where it touched the pad of the harness and was not covered by his overcoats, was getting painfully cold, especially when the horse walked slowly. His legs and arms trembled and his breathing came fast. He saw himself perishing amid this dreadful snowy waste, and could see no means of escape.

Suddenly the horse under him tumbled into something and, sinking into a snow-drift, began to plunge and fell on his side. Vasíli Andréevich jumped off, and in so doing dragged to one side the breechband on which his foot was resting, and twisted round the pad to which he held as he dismounted. As soon as he had jumped off, the horse struggled to his feet, plunged forward, gave one leap and another, neighed again, and dragging the drugget and the breechband after him, disappeared, leaving Vasíli Andréevich alone in the snow-drift.

The latter pressed on after the horse, but the snow lay so deep and his coats were so heavy that, sinking above his knees at each step, he stopped breathless after taking not more than twenty steps. "The copse, the oxen, the leasehold, the shop, the tavern, the house with the iron-roofed barn, and my heir," thought he. "How can I leave all that? What does this mean? It cannot be!" These thoughts flashed through his mind. Then he thought of the wormwood tossed by the wind, which he had twice ridden past, and he was seized with such terror that he did not believe in the reality of what was happening to him. "Can this be a dream?" he thought, and tried to wake up but could not. It was real snow that lashed his face and covered him and chilled his right hand from which he had lost the glove, and this was a real desert in which he was now left alone like that wormwood, awaiting an inevitable, speedy, and meaningless death.

"Queen of Heaven! Holy Father Nicholas, teacher of temperance!" he thought, recalling the service of the day before and the holy icon with its black face and gilt frame, and the tapers which he sold to be set before that icon and which were almost immediately brought back to him scarcely burnt at all, and which he put away in the store-chest.[1] He began to pray to that same Nicholas the Wonder-Worker to save him, promising him a thanksgiving service and some candles. But he clearly and indubitably realized that the icon, its frame, the candles, the priest, and the thanksgiving service, though very important and necessary in church, could do nothing for him here, and that there was and could be no connection between those candles and services and his present disastrous plight. "I must not despair," he thought. "I must follow the horse's track before it is snowed under. He will lead me out, or I may even catch him. Only I must not hurry, or I shall stick fast and be more lost than ever."

But in spite of his resolution to go quietly, he rushed forward

[1] As churchwarden Vasíli Andréevich sold the tapers the worshippers bought to set before the icons. These were collected at the end of the service, and could afterwards be resold to the advantage of the church revenue.

216

and even ran, continually falling, getting up and falling again. The horse's track was already hardly visible in places where the snow did not lie deep. "I am lost!" thought Vasíli Andréevich. "I shall lose the track and not catch the horse." But at that moment he saw something black. It was Mukhórty, and not only Mukhórty, but the sledge with the shafts and the kerchief. Mukhórty, with the drugget and the breechband twisted round to one side, was standing not in his former place but nearer to the shafts, shaking his head which the reins he was stepping on drew downwards. It turned out that Vasíli Andréevich had sunk in the same ravine Nikíta had previously fallen into, and that Mukhórty had been bringing him back to the sledge and he had got off his back no more than fifty paces from where the sledge was.

IX

Having stumbled back to the sledge Vasíli Andréevich caught hold of it and for a long time stood motionless, trying to calm himself and recover his breath. Nikíta was not in his former place, but something, already covered with snow, was lying in the sledge and Vasíli Andréevich concluded that this was Nikíta. His terror had now quite left him, and if he felt any fear it was lest the dreadful terror should return that he had experienced when on the horse and especially when he was left alone in the snow-drift. At any cost he had to avoid that terror, and to keep it away he must do something—occupy himself with something. And the first thing he did was to turn his back to the wind and open his fur coat. Then, as soon as he recovered his breath a little, he shook the snow out of his boots and out of his left-hand glove (the right-hand glove was hopelessly lost and by this time probably lying somewhere under a dozen inches of snow), then as was his custom when going out of his shop to buy grain from the peasants, he pulled his girdle low down and

217

tightened it and prepared for action. The first thing that occurred to him was to free Mukhórty's leg from the reins. Having done that, and tethered him to the iron cramp at the front of the sledge where he had been before, he was going round the horse's quarters to put the breechband and pad straight and cover him with the cloth, but at that moment he noticed that something was moving in the sledge and Nikíta's head rose up out of the snow that covered it. Nikíta, who was half frozen, rose with great difficulty and sat up, moving his hand before his nose in a strange manner just as if he were driving away flies. He waved his hand and said something, and seemed to Vasíli Andréevich to be calling him. Vasíli Andréevich left the cloth unadjusted and went up to the sledge.

"What is it?" he asked. "What are you saying?"

"I'm dy—ing, that's what," said Nikíta brokenly and with difficulty. "Give what is owing to me to my lad, or to my wife, no matter."

"Why, are you really frozen?" asked Vasíli Andréevich.

"I feel it's my death. Forgive me for Christ's sake . . ." said Nikíta in a tearful voice, continuing to wave his hand before his face as if driving away flies.

Vasíli Andréevich stood silent and motionless for half a minute. Then suddenly, with the same resolution with which he used to strike hands when making a good purchase, he took a step back and turning up his sleeves began raking the snow off Nikíta and out of the sledge. Having done this he hurriedly undid his girdle, opened out his fur coat, and having pushed Nikíta down, lay down on top of him, covering him not only with his fur coat but with the whole of his body, which glowed with warmth. After pushing the skirts of his coat between Nikíta and the sides of the sledge, and holding down its hem with his knees, Vasíli Andréevich lay like that face down, with his head pressed against the front of the sledge. Here he no longer heard

218

the horse's movements or the whistling of the wind, but only Nikíta's breathing. At first and for a long time Nikíta lay motionless, then he sighed deeply and moved.

"There, and you say you are dying! Lie still and get warm, that's our way . . ." began Vasíli Andréevich.

But to his great surprise he could say no more, for tears came to his eyes and his lower jaw began to quiver rapidly. He stopped speaking and only gulped down the risings in his throat. "Seems I was badly frightened and have gone quite weak," he thought. But this weakness was not only not unpleasant, but gave him a peculiar joy such as he had never felt before.

"That's our way!" he said to himself, experiencing a strange and solemn tenderness. He lay like that for a long time, wiping his eyes on the fur of his coat and tucking under his knee the right skirt, which the wind kept turning up.

But he longed so passionately to tell somebody of his joyful condition that he said: "Nikíta!"

"It's comfortable, warm!" came a voice from beneath.

"There, you see, friend, I was going to perish. And you would have been frozen, and I should have. . . ."

But again his jaws began to quiver and his eyes to fill with tears, and he could say no more.

"Well, never mind," he thought. "I know about myself what I know."

He remained silent and lay like that for a long time.

Nikíta kept him warm from below and his fur coats from above. Only his hands, with which he kept his coat-skirts down round Nikíta's sides, and his legs which the wind kept uncovering, began to freeze, especially his right hand which had no glove. But he did not think of his legs or of his hands but only of how to warm the peasant who was lying under him. He looked out several times at Mukhórty and could see that his back was uncovered and the drugget and breeching lying on the snow,

219

and that he ought to get up and cover him, but he could not bring himself to leave Nikíta and disturb even for a moment the joyous condition he was in. He no longer felt any kind of terror.

"No fear, we shan't lose him this time!" he said to himself, referring to his getting the peasant warm with the same boastfulness with which he spoke of his buying and selling.

Vasíli Andréevich lay in that way for one hour, another, and a third, but he was unconscious of the passage of time. At first impressions of the snowstorm, the sledge-shafts, and the horse with the shaft-bow shaking before his eyes, kept passing through his mind, then he remembered Nikíta lying under him, then recollections of the festival, his wife, the police-officer, and the box of candles, began to mingle with these; then again Nikíta, this time lying under that box, then the peasants, customers and traders, and the white walls of his house with its iron roof, with Nikíta lying underneath, presented themselves to his imagination. Afterwards all these impressions blended into one nothingness. As the colors of the rainbow unite into one white light, so all these different impressions mingled into one, and he fell asleep.

For a long time he slept without dreaming, but just before dawn the visions recommenced. It seemed to him that he was standing by the box of tapers and that Tíkhon's wife was asking for a five-kopék taper for the Church fete. He wished to take one out and give it to her, but his hands would not lift, being held tight in his pockets. He wanted to walk round the box but his feet would not move and his new clean goloshes had grown to the stone floor, and he could neither lift them nor get his feet out of the goloshes. Then the taper-box was no longer a box but a bed, and suddenly Vasíli Andréevich saw himself lying in his bed at home. He was lying in his bed and could not get up. Yet it was necessary for him to get up because Iván Matvéich, the police-officer, would soon call for him and he had to go with

220

him—either to bargain for the forest or to put Mukhórty's breeching straight.

He asked his wife: "Nikoláevna,[1] hasn't he come yet?" "No, he hasn't," she replied. He heard someone drive up to the front steps. "It must be him." "No, he's gone past." "Nikoláevna! I say, Nikoláevna, isn't he here yet?" "No." He was still lying on his bed and could not get up, but was always waiting. And this waiting was uncanny and yet joyful. Then suddenly his joy was completed. He whom he was expecting came; not Iván Matvéich, the police-officer, but someone else—yet it was he whom he had been waiting for. He came and called him; and it was he who had called him and told him to lie down on Nikíta. And Vasíli Andréevich was glad that that one had come for him.

"I'm coming!" he cried joyfully, and that cry awoke him, but woke him up not at all the same person he had been when he fell asleep. He tried to get up but could not, tried to move his arm and could not, to move his leg and also could not, to turn his head and could not. He was surprised but not at all disturbed by this. He understood that this was death, and was not at all disturbed by that either. He remembered that Nikíta was lying under him and that he had got warm and was alive, and it seemed to him that he was Nikíta and Nikíta was he, and that his life was not in himself but in Nikíta. He strained his ears and heard Nikíta breathing and even slightly snoring. "Nikíta is alive, so I too am alive!" he said to himself triumphantly.

And he remembered his money, his shop, his house, the buying and selling, and Mirónov's millions, and it was hard for him to understand why that man, called Vasíli Brekhunóv, had troubled himself with all those things with which he had been troubled.

"Well, it was because he did not know what the real thing was," he thought, concerning that Vasíli Brekhunóv. "He did

1 A familiar peasant use of the patronymic in place of the Christian name.

not know, but now I know and know for sure. Now I know!" And again he heard the voice of the one who had called him before. "I'm coming! Coming!" he responded gladly, and his whole being was filled with joyful emotion. He felt himself free and that nothing could hold him back any longer.

After that Vasíli Andréevich neither saw, heard, nor felt anything more in this world.

All around the snow still eddied. The same whirlwinds of snow circled about, covering the dead Vasíli Andréevich's fur coat, the shivering Mukhórty, the sledge, now scarcely to be seen, and Nikíta lying at the bottom of it, kept warm beneath his dead master.

X

Nikíta awoke before daybreak. He was aroused by the cold that had begun to creep down his back. He had dreamt that he was coming from the mill with a load of his master's flour and when crossing the stream had missed the bridge and let the cart get stuck. And he saw that he had crawled under the cart and was trying to lift it by arching his back. But strange to say the cart did not move, it stuck to his back and he could neither lift it nor get out from under it. It was crushing the whole of his loins. And how cold it felt! Evidently he must crawl out. "Have done!" he exclaimed to whoever was pressing the cart down on him. "Take out the sacks!" But the cart pressed down colder and colder, and then he heard a strange knocking, awoke completely, and remembered everything. The cold cart was his dead and frozen master lying upon him. And the knock was produced by Mukhórty, who had twice struck the sledge with his hoof.

"Andréevich! Eh, Andréevich!"[1] Nikíta called cautiously,

[1] Again the characteristic peasant use of the patronymic without the Christian name preceding it.

222

beginning to realize the truth, and straightening his back. But Vasíli Andréevich did not answer and his stomach and legs were stiff and cold and heavy like iron weights.

"He must have died! May the Kingdom of Heaven be his!" thought Nikíta.

He turned his head, dug with his hand through the snow about him and opened his eyes. It was daylight; the wind was whistling as before between the shafts, and the snow was falling in the same way, except that it was no longer driving against the frame of the sledge but silently covered both sledge and horse deeper and deeper, and neither the horse's movements nor his breathing were any longer to be heard.

"He must have frozen too," thought Nikíta of Mukhórty, and indeed those hoof knocks against the sledge, which had awakened Nikíta, were the last efforts the already numbed Mukhórty had made to keep on his feet before dying.

"O Lord God, it seems Thou art calling me too!" said Nikíta. "Thy Holy Will be done. But it's uncanny. . . . Still, a man can't die twice and must die once. If only it would come soon!"

And he again drew in his head, closed his eyes, and became unconscious, fully convinced that now he was certainly and finally dying.

It was not till noon that day that peasants dug Vasíli Andréevich and Nikíta out of the snow with their shovels, not more than seventy yards from the road and less than half a mile from the village.

The snow had hidden the sledge, but the shafts and the kerchief tied to them were still visible. Mukhórty, buried up to his belly in snow, with the breeching and drugget hanging down, stood all white, his dead head pressed against his frozen throat: icicles hung from his nostrils, his eyes were covered with hoar-

223

frost as though filled with tears, and he had grown so thin in that one night that he was nothing but skin and bone.

Vasíli Andréevich was stiff as a frozen carcass, and when they rolled him off Nikíta his legs remained apart and his arms stretched out as they had been. His bulging hawk eyes were frozen, and his open mouth under his clipped moustache was full of snow. But Nikíta though chilled through was still alive. When he had been brought to, he felt sure that he was already dead and that what was taking place with him was no longer happening in this world but in the next. When he heard the peasants shouting as they dug him out and rolled the frozen body of Vasíli Andréevich from off him, he was at first surprised that in the other world peasants should be shouting in the same old way and had the same kind of body, and then when he realized that he was still in this world he was sorry rather than glad, especially when he found that the toes on both his feet were frozen.

Nikíta lay in hospital for two months. They cut off three of his toes, but the others recovered so that he was still able to work and went on living for another twenty years, first as a farm-laborer, then in his old age as a watchman. He died at home as he had wished, only this year, under the icons with a lighted taper in his hands. Before he died he asked his wife's forgiveness and forgave her for the cooper. He also took leave of his son and grandchildren, and died sincerely glad that he was relieving his son and daughter-in-law of the burden of having to feed him, and that he was now really passing from this life of which he was weary into that other life which every year and every hour grew clearer and more desirable to him. Whether he is better or worse off there where he awoke after his death, whether he was disappointed or found there what he expected, we shall all soon learn.

1895.